Although he'd never expected to be part of raising a baby, Matt had fallen in love with Danny at first sight.

But while Matt was still learning how to clean up diapers and mix formula, there was a car accident and his brother—Danny's father—died.

And then it was just the two of them. An ill-prepared bachelor and a baby abandoned by his mother. That's when Matt made the promise he never intended to break.

And he'd built two cradles. One for the house, one for the shop. So he could watch over Danny, protect him. He would do anything, give anything to keep his boy safe. Even if it was from the child's own mother.

Books by Bonnie K. Winn

Love Inspired

A Family All Her Own #158
**Family Ties* #186
**Promise of Grace* #222
**Protected Hearts* #299
**Child of Mine* #348

*Rosewood, Texas

BONNIE K. WINN

is a hopeless romantic who's written incessantly since the third grade. So it seemed only natural that she turn to romance writing. A seasoned author of historical and contemporary romance, her bestselling books have won numerous awards. *Affaire de Coeur* chose her as one of the Top Ten Romance Writers in America.

Bonnie loves writing contemporary romance because she can set her stories in the modern cities close to her heart and explore the endlessly fascinating strengths of today's woman.

Living in the foothills of the Rockies gives her plenty of inspiration and a touch of whimsy, as well. She shares her life with her husband, son and a spunky Westie who lends his characteristics to many pets in her stories. Bonnie's keeping mum about anyone else's characteristics she may have borrowed.

CHILD OF MINE

BONNIE K. WINN

Published by Steeple Hill Books™

STEEPLE HILL BOOKS

ISBN 0-373-81262-0

CHILD OF MINE

This edition published by arrangement with Steeple Hill Books.

www.SteepleHill.com

Printed in U.S.A.

For Donna Hobbs, friend, sister, keeper of secrets, guardian of memories. You've been there for me through everything. We've shared weddings, babies, dreams and everything in between. I think often of the days we tunneled to lunch, walked to Sam Houston Park, the library. Our connection transcends the miles, but I miss you, dear friend.

Prologue

Los Angeles, California

The carton was small. But it was all Kyle had left behind when he'd disappeared eight years ago, taking their precious baby, stealing her hope.

Sitting cross-legged on the floor in the attic of her parents' Brentwood home, Leah Hunter dug through the contents of the carton as she had hundreds of times before. She'd tried to leave it behind when she moved to her own apartment. But she couldn't. She was searching for a clue, *any* clue that could tell her where Kyle had gone.

She had been nineteen when she'd married him. A naive nineteen, she realized now, because she'd believed Kyle's lies. But she'd never believed he would kidnap baby Danny.

Leah picked up the only unique item in the carton, a hand-carved box. It was so simple it was elegant. She opened the hinged lid and smoothed her fingers over the sleek wood interior, searching for a hidden panel—yet again. But she still couldn't find anything. Like everything else Kyle had left, it was a dead end.

She had been as dazzled by him as he'd been by her parents' money. It was all he'd ever wanted from her. But when they wouldn't hand out the money, he'd taken Danny.

Frustrated, Leah tapped on the side of the box fiercely. A small drawer, the same size as the base of the box, slid open.

Her heart skipped a beat. Shaking, she lifted it to the light.

The drawer was empty, but engraved on one side was a name: *Matt Whitaker.* And a place: *Rosewood, Texas.*

It could just be the name of the person who'd carved the box, Leah realized. But it was the first clue in eight years. And nothing would keep her from trying to find her son. Nothing.

Chapter One

Rosewood, Texas

Whitaker Woods. Like the box Leah clutched in her hand, the native pine storefront was simple. Pushing open the door, she expected to find small, similar pieces inside. She was surprised instead by the array of large furniture. Dramatic armoires, one-of-a-kind chairs, trunks, chests.

"Can I help you?" An older woman emerged from the back, the wood floor creaking beneath her.

"Yes." Hope crowding her throat, Leah showed her the box. "I'm trying to locate the sales record for this."

The woman wiped her freckled hands on the industrial apron she wore. "That I can't do."

Leah fought her disappointment.

"Matt only makes these for friends or family," she continued, picking up the box. "He doesn't sell them."

"Oh?"

She turned the box over. "Yes. They're special."

Leah seized the new information as if were gold. "Do you by chance know Kyle Johnson?"

"Kyle? No."

Leah hadn't really expected that she would. Still… "Could I speak to Mr. Whitaker?"

"Matt's not here right now. He'll probably be back in a few hours. I could have him call you."

"That would be great." Leah handed her a card. "This has my cell number. I'm staying at Borbey House just down the street."

"Annie's place. I know it."

Leah smiled. "Thanks for your help."

"Welcome to Rosewood."

* * *

Matt whistled as he unloaded the pickup truck. He was especially pleased with the custom hall tree he'd just finished. The concept was Victorian. The contemporary design, however, was all his own. He loved working with his hands. Always had. Bringing the wood from one life to another.

Easing the hall tree through the back door of the store, Matt was careful not to scratch the multiple layers of varnish.

"Boss, that you?"

"Yeah."

Nan walked through the swinging doors that separated the display area from the back room and spotted the hall tree. "Oh, that's nice!"

He stood back, surveying the piece. "I'm happy with it."

"Bet it doesn't last long. And you'll have a dozen requests for more."

"You're better than an ad in the *Houston Chronicle*."

Nan grinned. "Glad you noticed."

"How's the day been?"

"Steady. Cindy Mallory wants to talk to you about ordering some new furniture for the triplets. Sounds like a pretty big commission. And I sold that rocking chair I've had my eye on for my youngest daughter. Should have bought it myself when I had the chance."

He chuckled. "I told you to put it aside."

"Sold it to a tourist for full price, Matt."

"Not everything's about the bottom line."

"Good thing I take care of the books," she chided. "Oh, and a pretty young woman came by to see you."

"Ah...wish I'd been here."

"She had one of those special little boxes you make, wanted to see if I could trace it." Nan handed him Leah's card. "And she wanted to know if I knew a Kyle Johnson."

Matt froze.

"Told her that you just made them for special friends. She's staying over at Annie's place. Card has her cell number on it, too. Seemed nice enough. Funny though. Her having the box and not knowing they're special. But I told her I'd ask you to call." Nan paused. "Matt? You okay?"

"Yeah…sure."

"You never used to sell the little boxes, did you?"

"No. Uh…I'd better get back to the house."

"Well, okay. You sure everything's all right?"

"Yeah. Just been a long day."

Nan glanced at her watch. "It's just after two. You want some coffee?"

"No. You go ahead."

Back in his truck Matt studied the card. And eight years crashed away.

Sitting in an overstuffed chair that was so comfortable it should have lulled her into a nap, Leah stared at the phone in her room. A few hours, the clerk had said, before Matt Whitaker would return to the store. She'd unpacked and tried to fiddle away as much time as she could but she still had too much left on her hands. It would be awhile before he called. She pictured her mother back in L.A., anxiously waiting to hear if she had any news. Might as well let her know not to sit by the phone.

Rhonda picked up on the first ring. "Leah?"

"Hi, Mom."

"Have you found out anything?"

"Not yet, but I'm working on it."

"Maybe you should have let the investigators—"

"Not this time, Mom." Leah's jaw tensed. "I have to do this one on my own."

There was a pause. "Maybe you're right. The detectives never found out anything despite all their searching."

No. And though Leah had believed Kyle would bring Danny back, he hadn't. She sighed.

"We could contact the FBI again," Rhonda reminded her.

"It didn't work the last time."

Rhonda's silence told Leah her mother didn't appreciate the comeback. But the silence was short-lived. "How you could have been married to a man who left absolutely no record of his name…and for you to not have his social security number…"

Leah didn't have an answer. Kyle hadn't held a job while they were married and her mother knew it. And the FBI found that the background he'd told her was fiction—a fairy tale to make a gullible girl fall in love. Which gave them nothing to trace. "What do you want me to say?"

Rhonda must've tapped her rings against her desk, the sound coming clearly through the phone. "I don't suppose there's any point in going over old wounds."

What did it matter now? They'd already been scraped open. Leah rolled her eyes. She knew her mother was just anxious about Danny. But the woman was cranking her own anxiety level even higher. She struggled to keep her voice calm. "Is everything okay at work, Mom?" Hunter Design was a thriving L.A.-based design firm with an international clientele. Kyle had seen only dollar signs in the family-operated business. Her parents had been willing to hire him, but he hadn't wanted to work. He just wanted the money.

"Jennifer's keeping an eye on your jobs. She's competent, even if she doesn't have your touch."

Jennifer was Leah's assistant. "She'll be fine."

"Leah? Don't be too disappointed if this doesn't...well, turn into the lead you're hoping for."

"I won't, Mom."

Once she'd said goodbye to her mother, Leah glanced around the storybook room in the quaint bed-and-breakfast. She had been on hyper-speed since she'd found the secret compartment in the box and decided to pursue this long shot at finding Danny. On edge, she'd flown to Houston, rented a car and driven more than three hours to this small town, hidden in the heart of the Texas hill country. She'd heard it was a beautiful region, but she'd barely seen anything she'd driven past.

The thought of just sitting, without anything to do, was making her crazy.

Maybe she could walk off some of her nervous energy.

Stopping at the antique breakfront that served as a desk, Leah rang the bell. Annie, the B and B owner, popped out of the adjoining kitchen, wiping her hands on a cloth. She was more than happy to forward any messages to Leah's cell phone.

The air was clear, delivering early spring's promise of new life, as Leah walked down the old-fashioned boardwalk. Tall elm trees shaded the street. The buildings belonged to a different era, she realized. Enchanting Victorian structures, which all housed working businesses.

She passed a quaint drugstore, hardware store, costume shop and newspaper office before reaching Whitakers Woods. She lingered in front of the wide-paned window, but didn't see a man inside. The door opened and a customer stepped out.

The woman Leah had met earlier called out to her. "Hi, there!"

Leah walked inside. "Hello…"

"I'm Nan," she said with a smile.

"Should have introduced myself earlier. Matt was here sooner than I thought and I gave him your card."

"Great! Then I guess I'll be hearing from him soon."

Nan nodded. "Oh, my, yes. Matt's real good about getting back to people."

Relieved, Leah smiled. "That's wonderful. Thanks for your help."

"Glad to do it. You settling in at Annie's?"

"Yes. It's a charming place. Like the town."

"Thing is, it's a real town, not put on for tourists like some places. No T-shirt and souvenir shops. Not that we don't welcome visitors, but this is our home."

"I got that sense right away."

"Good. Hope you have a nice stay."

Leah crossed her fingers. "I'm counting on it."

Matt sat at his kitchen table staring at Leah's card. It had to be her. It all fit. L.A. The box John had taken from him…along with Matt's savings.

"Kyle" she'd called him. Kyle Johnson.

His half brother had always hated his real name. John Litchkyl Johnson. Litchkyl, their mother's maiden name. He'd been John all his life in Rosewood. His hick life, he'd called it. He must have gone by Kyle once he'd gotten to California and married Leah.

But why was she here now?

She'd abandoned John and their baby when Danny was only six weeks old. What kind of woman did that? Only the lowest kind.

And she had money, John had said. Enough to have hired nannies, people to help out, to make raising her child as easy as possible. Instead she'd left. Said she didn't want the responsibility of a kid.

Matt could still feel the weight of that tiny bundle in his arms the first time he'd held Danny, the clutch of little fingers around his own. The promise he'd made.

He knew John had his faults. His half brother had been immature, irresponsible. But he also knew that a child belonged with his parents. At least the one who cared enough to stay with him. John had abandoned his own dreams of making it in California to come back to Rosewood where his only family remained. Their mother had passed on when John was sixteen, and John's father had died years before. Matt was all he had left.

And though he'd never expected to be part of raising a baby, Matt had fallen in love with Danny at first sight. That had never changed.

But the family dynamics *had* changed almost immediately. While Matt was still learning how to clean up diapers and mix formula, there was the car accident.

And then it was just the two of them. An ill-prepared bachelor and a motherless child. That's when Matt made the promise he never intended to break.

And he'd built two cradles. One for the house, one for the shop. So he could watch over Danny, protect him. That wasn't going to stop. He would do anything, give anything to keep his boy safe. Even if it meant taking over as the only father Danny would ever remember. Oh, he'd tell Danny the truth when he was old enough to under-

Chapter Two

"Are you sure there aren't any messages for me?" Leah asked.

Annie shook her head. "I'm sorry. I double-checked. If I'm out, I have an answering machine. Locals are usually pretty good about leaving messages. I can't be as sure about out-of-towners..."

"It's local. Whitaker Woods."

"Oh, they're really good about getting back to you." Annie smiled. "Matt's stuff is special, isn't it? People find out about his furniture, drive up here from all over. Usually Nan is at the store most of the time, though."

"Actually, I need to speak to Mr. Whitaker."

"I'm surprised he hasn't followed up with you since yesterday." Annie glanced at the clock. It was after seven. "Wow. It's been a day and a half. That's really not like him. Have you talked to Nan?"

"Repeatedly. Seems he's out on a commission job."

Annie nodded sympathetically. "Matt works like an artist, gets all caught up in what he does." She pointed across the room. "See that bench? He recreated it from some fuzzy old photos for my grandfather. Took great care with every detail. The original was lost in a fire. It was a wedding present to Gramps from my great-grandparents. And it meant so much to him when Matt was able to make another one. He said it brought Granny closer to him those last years." Annie cleared her throat. "Anyway, like I said, Matt becomes really caught up in his projects."

Leah understood, but it wasn't getting her any closer to talking with him. "Thanks anyway."

Climbing the stairs back to her room, she couldn't help but wonder. Matt usually got back to people quickly. So, why wasn't he getting back to her?

At breakfast the next morning, Leah dawdled over her French toast.

"Do you want another slice?" Annie offered.

"No, thanks. It's delicious, but I shouldn't be eating anything this rich for breakfast."

Annie chuckled. "The guests usually say that. But they rarely order anything else after they try it. It was my grandmother's recipe."

"I'm guessing you were close to your grandparents."

"This was their place. The one that *didn't* burn down." Annie lifted the coffee-pot. "More coffee?"

"Since I'm the last one in the dining room, why don't you join me, unless I'm keeping you from something?"

"Best offer I've had all morning."

Leah added more cream to her cup. "Do

you ever get tired of having your house full of people?"

Annie hesitated. "You'd think so, wouldn't you?"

"Actually, I've been considering combining work and home spaces—I'm a designer."

"Really? That must be interesting."

"I like it. But then I kind of fell into it. It's my family's business. A third-generation business."

"Like mine. This was a bakery during my grandparents' time."

"So you know what I mean. I grew up playing with fabric and paint. I thought sample books were toys."

Annie grinned. "I'd have loved that. I've always wanted to do something more with this place."

"It's beautiful. Fits perfectly with the period of the building, of the town actually."

"Thanks. For the most part, these were my grandparents' furnishings. They used this room for the display area so it was a natural for the dining room. But I'd like to put my stamp on another room."

"It's the woman in us," Leah commiserated.

"True."

Leah sipped her coffee. "Do you know if Whitaker's combines its workshop and retail space?"

"Hmm? Oh, there's a work space at the store, but Matt does most of his work at the shop behind his house."

"Did you have a particular room in mind to redo, Annie?" Leah asked, picking up on her earlier comment.

"One the public doesn't have access to, I think," she mused. "Maybe my bedroom."

For a few minutes they talked about Annie's decorating wish list. Leah didn't want to rush the conversation, but at some point she intended to ask Annie just where the Whitaker house was.

If Matt Whitaker wouldn't call her, she would have to call on him.

The rambling two-story house was old, well kept and surprisingly cozy-looking. It also appeared to be empty.

First, Leah rang the bell at the front door. Then waited. Then rang it again. And again.

She tried knocking.

She tried the back door.

Not thwarted, she searched out the shop. A tall, wide double door stood open. Apparently theft wasn't an issue in this part of the world.

She found nothing but wood and tools in the orderly, pine-scented shop. She breathed in the smell of newly cut timber and wood dust, but they didn't tell her if Whitaker had been there that day or even that week. She suspected the shop always smelled of freshly cut wood.

Going back to the house, she took out a card, scribbled a message on the back—explaining that she urgently needed to speak to him—and tucked it in the space by the front door.

Leah considered camping out until Matt Whitaker returned, but who knew when that would be?

So she checked again at the store. Nan was apologetic, assuring her that Matt would be in touch at some point.

She waited at Borbey House until after five o'clock and drove out to the Whitaker house again. No one was home.

Frustrated, she returned to the bed-and-breakfast.

Annie was tidying the parlor. "Any luck?"

"None." Disheartened, she started climbing the stairs.

"Wait." Annie put down her feather duster. "I know it's exasperating, I mean, you driving all this way, not being able to get in touch with Matt. Why don't you come with me this evening to the church supper? It's always fun. We have games afterward."

Leah was about to refuse. "And Matt might be there."

That clinched it for her. "Oh? Are you sure I won't be in the way?"

"At our church? Never. It's a potluck and we always have plenty of food and then some."

Annie was about Leah's age, and her lively dark eyes were warm and inviting. But Leah didn't want to take advantage. "Then, can I make a donation?"

"It's not necessary. Really, everyone's welcome."

"Hmm. I couldn't help noticing that you make a lot of extra pies."

"This *is* Borbey House—Hungarian for 'baker.' Selling the pies is a holdover tradition from the days when my grandparents ran the bakery."

"Good. I'd like to buy two, please."

Annie grinned. "Hungry, are we?"

"I'll let you pick the flavors." Leah glanced down at her jeans and frowned. "I didn't bring a dress."

"You look about the same size as me. I'll loan you something."

"Really?"

"It won't be a designer label, but if that doesn't bother you…"

"Annie, you redefine hospitality."

Rosewood Community Church was located in a beautiful old building. Annie explained that the structure had sustained an electrical fire that had nearly wiped it out a few years earlier. But the membership had come together to rebuild. By using some of the original stones, they had maintained the best of the past, while making sure they had a future.

Leah listened as she clenched and unclenched her sweaty hands, studying the people around them. She leaned close to Annie. "What does Matt Whitaker look like?"

"Um…tall, early thirties, dark brown hair that's kind of sun-streaked…" She paused. "You know he works with lots of wood and tools, so he's fit, muscular. Casual dresser. What did I leave out?"

Leah shook her head. "Not much." But she couldn't stop staring at every man who passed by.

She didn't pay much attention to the tables of food, although she followed Annie's lead and filled her plate, then took a seat. The people were friendly, introducing themselves. She was surprised by their welcome. It was so different than being in the city.

"There's Matt. About two tables over on the left." Annie pointed tactfully. "See? Next to that family?"

Leah was relieved to finally see him. She'd begun to think that even in such a small town she wasn't going to catch up to him. Although she wanted to pin him down now, manners kept her from bothering him until he finished his dinner.

A man and woman sitting at the table between hers and his stood up, clearing her view. It was then she saw the young boy at Matt's side. A boy that looked to be about the same age Danny would be. Leah swallowed.

She always noticed young boys, wondering how her own son had turned out. Still… She watched father and son together. Their postures were nearly identical. Their gestures similar. Matt paid careful attention to the boy.

"Dessert, Leah?" Annie asked.

"No, thanks."

"There's a cheesecake over there calling out to me. I don't want to be rude, so I think I'll go answer."

"Mmm."

Annie shrugged and walked over to the dessert table.

Leah watched Matt Whitaker and the child. Although she couldn't hear what they were saying, the two heads were bent together and she could see the boy's grin, Matt's quick smile.

They were close. It was evident in the easy body language, the looks they exchanged.

Surely a man who loved his son this much would understand her quest.

As Leah watched, the boy jumped up from the table, hugged Matt and then ran to join the other kids his age in the games that were beginning. Leah found it difficult to take her gaze from him, watching until he and the other children left the fellowship hall with a basketball, probably to go to the gymnasium.

Annie had returned with her cheesecake, extra happy that she'd found chocolate sauce to go with it. She urged Leah to go over to see Matt.

He was still at the table, finishing his meal, when she approached.

"Mr. Whitaker?"

He glanced up.

"I'm Leah Hunter."

His expression turned wary. "Yes?"

"I've been trying to reach you at your store. Sorry to ambush you here." Leah smiled, trying to take the businesslike edge from her words. "I'm with Annie. I mean, she invited me to the church supper, being a stranger in town and all."

Not a word from him.

"And me being at loose ends," Leah continued, filling in the awkward silence. "I wasn't planning to be in Rosewood long. I just came to talk to you. I think Nan gave you my card."

The silence was so protracted she wondered if he would speak.

When he finally did, his voice was deep, somber. "She gave it to me."

Which told her nothing. "So…" Leah studied his unblinking gaze. "I'm trying to trace down a box I have—"

"Nan told you we don't keep records on the boxes."

"She said you only make the boxes for family or special friends—"

"Miss Hunter, my friends don't sell their boxes."

"I didn't say I'd bought it."

"You've come a long way for nothing then." He stood, stepping aside and pushing his chair up to the table.

"No, Mr. Whitaker, I haven't." She pulled the box from her purse. "This is the first clue I've had to finding my son in eight years and you're not going to just dismiss me." She held it up. "This belonged to Kyle Johnson. Did you know him?"

His expression was at first startled, then guarded. His lips thin, pressed tightly together. One word finally emerged, as though it were painful to say. "Yes."

Her hope, thready at best, flared. She bit her lower lip to stave off tears. "Oh, Mr. Whitaker, you don't know what this means to me." Despite her effort, one tear slipped down her cheek and she wiped it away. "Where can I find him? I know he's difficult to pin down."

"Not anymore."

"No?"

"He's dead."

Chapter Three

Reeling, Leah stared at Matt's back as he walked away. She'd never let herself believe Kyle could be dead. Because if he were, that meant…

But the investigators had never found Kyle's death certificate. Whitaker had to be wrong.

"Wait! Please!" She ran to catch up to him. "When did Kyle die?"

He stopped and turned to her, his words clipped. "Eight years ago."

She gasped. Shaking, she felt the last remnants of her self-control slip away. "That can't be. We've been checking for years and never found a death certificate."

"His first name was John. Kyle was part of his middle name—Litchkyl."

All of Kyle's lies. Even his name. He'd signed their marriage certificate as Kyle Johnson. He'd cheapened every single thing about their marriage.

She closed her eyes, afraid to ask. Hope and despair warred in her heart. Swallowing, she lifted her chin. "And the baby? The boy?"

He hesitated.

And her heart nearly stopped.

"Is safe."

"Where is he?"

Matt stared at her.

"Please, if you know anything." She took a deep breath. "I'm sorry. I haven't explained myself very well. I was married to Kyle. The baby, the boy, I mean, is mine. I've been looking for him. That's why I'm here, why I'm trying to trace the box. So, if you can tell me anything..."

"It's too late. You made your choice."

She gaped at him. *Where did he get off...?* "I understand loyalty to a deceased friend, but you don't understand the circumstances—"

"I understand plenty."

There was derision in his tone, but she had no idea why. "I don't know what Kyle told you—"

"The truth."

She shook her head. "His version. Despite what he may have said, I need to find my son. You're a father. You must understand that."

"I understand you walked away once. Do the best thing for your son again. Walk away now."

Stunned, Leah watched as Matt Whitaker crossed the room and headed out the door.

Back at the bed-and-breakfast, Leah sat in one of the overstuffed chairs near her bedroom window. She still couldn't believe Matt Whitaker's reaction. And she never would have imagined that Kyle could elicit such loyalty.

Kyle dead. For all her anger, it wasn't something she would have wished. He'd been so young.

Who was raising her son? Had he been legally adopted?

Throat dry, she considered the possibilities—along with Matt Whitaker's harsh response. Getting his help wasn't going to be easy. But she would really need it to find Danny, especially if there'd been a private adoption. That wasn't something that could be simply traced.

Staring out at the quiet street, she knew she wouldn't sleep that night. Her mind was filled with too many questions.

Leah watched for Whitaker's truck. From her vantage point at the parlor window in the bed-and-breakfast, she could see the traffic going down Main Street.

Persistence paid off by midafternoon. As soon as he parked in front of his store, Leah bounded outside and down the boardwalk.

Matt was alone in the display area, his back to her. "Be with you in a minute."

"Fine."

He stiffened and turned around slowly.

"Mr. Whitaker…Matt, please, let me tell

you about my relationship with Kyle… John."

"I know all I need to."

"Obviously not, or you wouldn't be shutting me out. I was nineteen years old when we got married. I believed everything he told me—"

The bell over the door clanged as it opened. A group of young boys piled in, talking and laughing. The one she recognized as Whitaker's son ran up to him.

"Dad! Billy's dad's gonna take everybody for pizza after soccer practice. Can I go?"

Distracted, Matt glanced down at him. "Who's driving?"

"Billy and Dustin's dads. Is it okay?"

Leah watched the boy, able to see him close-up for the first time. He was animated, eager. Then he turned and she could see his face more clearly. As she studied his features, she saw that his eyes were a unique shade of green, like her own. Even their shape was similar to hers. So was his mouth. He looked up at her and the impact of recognition hit her.

Matt glanced at her, then down at his son. "It's all right, but home right after the pizza. And mind Billy's and Dustin's dads."

"Okay," the boy agreed. "Thanks, Dad."

"Come on, Danny," the others called.

Leah shivered as she watched him dash out with his friends. She'd been almost certain when she saw his eyes. The name confirmed it.

No wonder Matt had been avoiding her, putting her off. It all made sense. Perfect, horrible sense.

Anger, hot and raw, clawed through her. "How could you?" She turned on Matt with every bit of righteous pain and accusation she could muster. "I've heard of slime like you. How could you steal my child and then have the gall to pretend that you didn't know where he was?"

"Steal? Just how is it a person *steals* an abandoned baby? You're a real piece of work. What? Did you decide after eight years that it might be fun to play mommy? Forget it. Danny's done just fine without you until now. Go with your original instincts. Pretend he doesn't exist."

"Abandoned?" Leah shrieked. "Abandoned?"

"Boss, is everything okay in here?" Nan rushed in from the rear entrance. "I just got back from the post office and it sounds like someone's plucking live turkeys. You can hear it all the way outside."

Breathing hard, Leah and Matt paused.

"Yeah," Matt said in the awkward silence. Then he slammed out the door, got in his truck and roared away.

Leah was left in the heavy silence.

Embarrassed, Nan cleared her throat. "Sorry to interrupt."

"No. If anyone should apologize, it's me, I was the one yelling." Leah tried to calm her breathing. "Will you tell me one thing?"

"If I can."

"Did you know a John Johnson?"

"John? Sure. He was Matt's younger brother. Half brother, really. Matt was always looking out for him."

And still was, apparently.

Leah allowed enough time to collect herself before driving to Matt's house. His truck was parked out front. He didn't answer the door, so she walked around back to the shop.

He was sitting at his work bench, a piece of alder wood in his hands. Although she was sure he heard her, he didn't stir.

And she didn't bother with greetings. "You could have told me about Kyle being your brother."

"It didn't take you long to figure it out."

"I shouldn't have had to."

Matt put the wood down on the bench. "Why would you want to come back now? You're a stranger to Danny."

That stung. Badly. "Through no fault of my own. Kyle wanted money from my parents. They expected him to work for it. That wasn't in his plans, so he took Danny. Then he called and asked for half a million dollars. He said it was to set him up in his own business. He wanted to be a big-time real estate mogul just when the market was hitting bottom. My parents refused. I thought he'd give up and bring Danny home, but he didn't."

"I don't believe you."

"Danny was an infant! Barely six weeks old."

Matt met her gaze. "I'm the one who fed him. Changed his diapers. Rocked him to sleep. Held him when he cried."

Leah's chest constricted. "You think I didn't want to?"

"No."

"Because Kyle, who lied about everything, told you so?"

Matt stood. "You knew him, what? A year? I knew him all his life."

"Then you should have known he was chasing one half-baked idea after another. He didn't care about family, about establishing a real life together. All he wanted was a great big handout from my parents, and when that didn't happen he stole my son."

"He was pursuing his dreams, which he gave up to raise his son when you abandoned him."

She shook her head. "You can't really believe that."

"Because you say it isn't true?"

"I'm his mother."

"Which hasn't meant squat."

"This isn't going to end with your say-so. Danny is my son. That means legally, no matter what steps you may have taken."

"So you'll just rip him away from everything and everyone he knows and loves without a qualm."

Leah swallowed. "I know my rights."

"Kyle said that money ruled your conscience."

She gasped. "That isn't true."

"Then think about Danny instead of yourself." He walked toward her.

Automatically, Leah took a step backward.

Matt continued advancing. "He's not a baby anymore. He'll ask questions. About where you were."

"I'll tell him the truth."

Matt scoffed. "And he'll believe *you?* Why?"

"Because I'm his mother." Even as she spoke, Leah recognized the futility of the words. Danny didn't feel any connection to her. He would believe Matt. "You're not going to dissuade me." She could feel the pressure, the tightening in her chest, the ache against the back of her throat. But she wouldn't give into tears in front of this man. "I'll be back."

Trying to look as though she were still in control, she fled before her emotions exploded. Back in the car, she drove only a short distance from his house before she pulled off the road onto a deserted cattle crossing. Then she let the tears flow. Ugly, painful sobs clutched her chest and scraped her throat.

Her baby.

He didn't know her. He thought she'd tossed him aside. How was she going to fix that? And how was she going to explain that she had to take him away from the only parent he'd ever known?

Chapter Four

Leah picked at her oatmeal the following morning. She'd considered calling her parents' attorney, but Matt Whitaker's words echoed through her mind.

Then it occurred to her that she had only his version of how Danny had arrived in Rosewood.

"More coffee?" Annie asked.

"Thanks."

"You're awfully quiet. Everything okay?"

Leah glanced around the dining room and saw that the only other guests remaining, an older couple, were gathering their things to leave for the day. "Not really."

"I'm sorry. Anything I can do?"

"Do you have a minute?"

"Sure."

Annie put the coffeepot on the sideboard, waved goodbye to the other guests and joined her.

Leah twisted the linen napkin, wondering how to begin.

Annie waited patiently.

"I need to know something."

"I'll tell you if I can."

"Did you know John Johnson?"

Annie nodded. "Yes. It's been a long time. He died…I'm not sure…seems like almost ten years ago."

"Do you know anything about his child?"

She sighed. "Saddest thing. John met a girl in California. They got married and had a baby, but she ran out on him when the baby was just tiny. So John brought the baby back here, but he got killed in a car crash not long after he came home. His brother raised the boy like he was his own. He's Matt Whitaker—the man you came here to talk to." Her eyes widened.

Leah lowered her chin. "Is that what the whole town believes?"

Annie nodded slowly. "Leah?"

"Yes. I'm the girl. But it's not true." She looked into Annie's honest eyes. "I need someone to trust."

"I can keep your confidences...but, Leah, you have to know...the town feels really strongly about this. Everyone backs Matt. They admire how he took in the baby."

"But they don't know the truth."

"It's the truth everyone's lived with for nearly a decade," Annie reminded her gently. "Even if it wasn't true to begin with, it's going to be hard to convince people otherwise, especially after seeing a big strong guy like Matt with a baby. He's raised Danny by himself.... He never married."

Leah's heart caught as she thought of all the time she'd missed, all the firsts, all the accomplishments.

"Do you want to tell me about it?"

So Leah told her.

"John wasn't exactly wild," Annie remembered. "But he didn't run with my kind of crowd. He was a year ahead in school, but I remember he was different. Actually, I can see him taking off for California. So, if you didn't abandon Danny, that means you have legal rights."

"Yes."

"But if you take him away from everything he knows…"

Leah sighed heavily.

"If it helps," Annie said, "Matt seems to be a great father."

"I'm not sure it does. Of course, I wouldn't want to know Danny had been miserable. But his relationship with Matt complicates everything. I've always known that if I found him, it wouldn't be simple. But the reality is a lot harder than I ever imagined." And Leah was longing to put her arms around her little boy, to hug him close, to tell him that he was hers…to let him know how much she loved him. Instead, she sat drinking coffee, not even sure where he went to school.

Annie plucked the petals from one of the daisies on the table. "There's another way."

Leah met her gaze.

"Stay here in Rosewood. Get to know Danny. Establish some trust before you tell him who you are."

"Do you think Matt would let that happen?"

"I've seen Matt with him. I don't think he could hurt Danny by telling him the truth right now."

For all the other objections Leah might have about Matt, she couldn't deny his love for Danny.

She would do what it took to restore her maternal rights to her son, to convince Danny that she loved him. "Thank you, Annie. You've got a full-time guest."

Leah learned that Danny attended the Community Church's elementary school. No wonder his name had never appeared in public school records. Then she found out that he went by Danny Whitaker. In a small-town private school, a birth certificate hadn't been necessary, she guessed.

Or maybe Matt had taken the legal steps and adopted him.

She didn't have the heart to find that out just yet.

Instead, she decided to put her design skills to their best use. She made an appointment with the principal, explained that she was taking a break from her stressful job in L.A. but would love to volunteer at the school to give herself something to do while in Rosewood.

"Miss Hunter, we'd be delighted to have you," Principal Gunderland said after their meeting. She was taking Leah to see the lounge she had agreed to work on.

"Leah. And I'm pleased that I can be of help."

"An actual designer to help redecorate our teachers' lounge. The last time we tried to do anything with the room, we wound up painting it ghastly pink. No one liked it, so we repainted it institutional green, which is just as awful, maybe worse."

"I'll try for something a little more aesthetically pleasing," Leah murmured, struggling not to be obvious as she peeked into the classrooms they were passing.

"Don't take this the wrong way, but we'll be thrilled with anything."

Leah spotted a room full of children who looked to be about the right age, but she didn't see Danny among them. She needed to know what grade he was in. "Um…anything?"

"As long as it's in keeping with the church school."

Leah glanced into another classroom. "Of course. Tasteful, I understand."

"Mr. Whitaker!" the principal said in a delighted voice.

"Whitaker?" Leah echoed, jerking her gaze back to see Matt stalking down the hall toward them.

"Yes, he's one of our best supporters and volunteers."

Of course.

And he was glowering at her.

"Mr. Whitaker, is something wrong?" Principal Gunderland asked. "I saw the new bookcase in the library. It looks wonderful."

"Good."

The principal seemed surprised by his

curt reply. "Oh, this is Miss Hunter. She's a new volunteer, and you won't believe it—she's a professional designer!"

Leah smiled sweetly.

"We've met," he muttered.

"Then you know how lucky we are to have her," she exclaimed.

"Yeah, lucky."

"Miss Hunter, you'll be working quite a bit with Mr. Whitaker since he coordinates most of our redecorating."

The school secretary came hurrying up to them. There was an important call for the principal.

"Mr. Whitaker, would you mind escorting Miss Hunter to the teachers' lounge?" Mrs. Gunderland asked. "I'll meet you there in a few minutes."

He could hardly leave her there like a lump of hot coal, Leah realized, but she could tell he was seething as the two women walked away.

"What are you doing here?" Matt asked as he led her into the lounge.

"Checking out my son's school."

"How did you find out this is Danny's school?"

"It was hardly rocket science. Rosewood's a pretty small town. There aren't too many choices."

Matt wasn't satisfied. "Did you bring investigators to town?"

"Professionals wouldn't have stumbled around for two days to find out about Danny."

"I don't want you here."

"You don't have any choice."

"I could pull Danny out of this school."

"From everything he knows and enjoys?" she replied evenly.

"So, what? You're going to play at this until you get bored again?"

Leah wanted to shake him. "No. I'm going to stay in Rosewood until I get to know my son better."

"You won't last a week. This isn't L.A. We don't have fancy boutiques or clubs."

"You don't know me, Whitaker. Not everyone from L.A. is a party girl."

He snorted.

"I don't spend my days shopping and

playing tennis," she informed him. "I have a job."

"Don't you need to get back to it?"

"I'm on a leave of absence."

Matt looked at her suspiciously. "Just like that?"

"It was easier because my parents own the firm," she admitted. "But that doesn't make my work any less of a real job."

"Sure."

"Look. I don't have to prove anything to you. You're the one who didn't bother to check out Kyle's story." She saw the principal heading back toward them. "This isn't the place for this discussion."

"This isn't the place for *you*."

Leah kept a grip on her temper.

"So, what do you think of our teachers' lounge?" the principal asked, huffing a bit as she hurried toward them.

Leah hadn't even glanced at the room. Now that she did, she realized the principal was right. The lounge was ghastly.

"It could use some tender loving care."

Mrs. Gunderland laughed. "Said diplomatically. Don't you think so, Mr. Whitaker?"

Leah gave him her attention, too, just to needle him.

He noticed.

"We haven't done anything to the lounge since it was painted," he replied.

Avoiding the question, she noticed.

"We don't have much of a budget for redecorating," Mrs. Gunderland apologized.

"I have access to overrun materials through my work. Most I can get just for shipping costs." Leah thought of all the extra stock in the warehouse. Her parents would be happy to donate what was needed for a good cause. "There shouldn't be a problem."

The principal brightened. "Wow, you truly are an answer to prayer."

Leah thought of all her searching, all the years of wondering if she'd ever find Danny. "Thanks. That's how I feel about being here, too."

The following day Leah stretched out her time at the school, making different sketches of the teachers' lounge until recess. When the bell rang and the classes were dismissed, she watched eagerly until she finally spotted Danny filing out of his classroom.

Although he stayed in line as he was instructed, she could see the restrained energy, the animation she'd noticed before. She absorbed every detail. His hair was dark brown like Kyle's had been, but with the same sun streaks as Matt's. And he had freckles.

She swallowed. Silly. Freckles shouldn't make her come unglued.

But they were so precious.

And his eyes. They'd been so easy to recognize because they were like hers and like her father's.

Leah smiled, imagining Leland Hunter as a child, imagining him with his grandson.

Danny was a beautiful child, just as she'd known he would be. And he seemed so happy, easily smiling, laughing. Matt was right about one thing. She couldn't take him away.

But he was wrong about her commitment. She would last far more than a week. She would last as long as it took.

Chapter Five

"Dad? Where's Timbuktu?" Danny asked, sitting at the kitchen table, doing his homework.

Matt chuckled. "Where'd you hear about Timbuktu?"

"At school. Miss Randolph said that's where she's gonna go on her next vacation."

"I think Miss Randolph was joking. How many more reading questions do you have?"

"Two."

Miss Randolph must have been having a bad day, but kids could drive the most patient adult batty. Matt remembered when

Danny was about three, an age when he was questioning everything. He went through a period of asking about everyone he saw. Everyone they passed on the street, walking or driving. And even though Rosewood was a small town, that was a lot of "who's that?" Matt smiled to himself. But the little guy had been so excited to see every new face.

Every stage had been a revelation to Matt. He'd seen the world through new eyes.

Danny put his books and notebook into his backpack, then hung it on the hook near the door.

In the adjoining great room, Matt sat on a thick rug that was anchored by a heavy coffee table. On it, he and Danny had assembled an elaborate dinosaur settlement. Danny joined him, but seemed preoccupied as he adjusted the volcano.

Matt hoped Leah hadn't said anything. "Something bothering you, pal?"

Danny shrugged. "Billy's gonna have a baby brother or sister."

Matt could hear the dejected note in his son's voice. "You don't sound very excited."

"Billy was my only friend like me. You know, who didn't have any brothers or sisters."

Matt sighed. "I see." In the past he'd told Danny that it took both a mother and father in a marriage for siblings. He had impressed upon him the value of family, the sanctity of marriage. But he didn't want to bring up the subject of Danny's mother right now. He'd always told Danny that he didn't know where she was. "Billy's always been a good friend to you, hasn't he?"

"Uh-huh."

"And he's happy about having a new brother or sister?"

Danny pushed a toy brontosaurus close to a tall, plastic palm tree. "Uh-huh."

"Then, how should a good friend feel for him?"

Danny was quiet for a while. "Happy?"

"Yes, even though that's not very easy. But, what do we know about the right thing to do?"

"That it's not always easy."

Matt leaned over to hug him, his heart

tightening. He believed everything he'd taught his son and what he was telling him now. But he also believed everything he'd told Leah Hunter. He couldn't let her snatch Danny away from everything he knew and loved until she tired of whatever she was playing at. For all John's failings, Matt couldn't accept that he would have lied about something so important.

John's father had been a weak man, but Matt and John's mother had been a woman of deep faith and strong values. And Matt was convinced that John would have matured into a responsible man had he lived.

"Dad, do you think you might get married sometime?"

Matt cleared his throat. There hadn't been much time for anyone in his life except Danny. And now… "I don't know," he replied honestly. "But I can't get married just so you'll have a little brother or sister. It has to be someone I love."

Danny's eyes were so serious. "Do you love anyone?"

"You betcha." Matt tousled his dark hair. "I love you, buddy."

Danny giggled. “I know *that!*”

“Good.” Matt reached across the table, adjusting one of the toy dinosaurs. “Your tyrannosaurus rex is about to eat that palm tree.”

“Nah! A rex doesn’t eat trees!”

Soon they were engrossed in the dinosaur valley and remained so until bath and bedtime. After a story and prayers, Matt tucked Danny in.

He looked so young as his eyelids grew heavy and he fought the last surrender to sleep. So young and innocent. How would it affect his son if he and Leah waged a legal battle over him?

Sighing, Matt smoothed the hair back on Danny’s forehead. He straightened the blanket, then turned the lamp off. But he left a small night-light on as he’d always done.

Back in the kitchen, he reached in the refrigerator for a Coke when he heard a quiet knock on the back door. Opening it, he was glad to see his old friend. “Hey, Roger.”

“It’s not story or bath time, is it?”

"Nope, Danny just got to sleep."

"Wish I hadn't missed seeing him, but I'm glad I'm not interrupting. Can I borrow your router?"

"Sure." Matt held up his can of cola. "Want something to drink?"

"Sounds good."

Matt pulled out another Coke and handed it to his friend. "I'm sorry I didn't bring that bookcase over today."

Roger shrugged as he straddled one of the bar stools. "I figured you got busy."

"I got paranoid."

Pausing midway in opening the soft drink, Roger glanced at his friend. "That doesn't sound like you."

"Danny's mother's in town."

"What?"

Matt took the stool across the counter. "No warning. Just showed up."

"What does she want?"

"Danny."

Roger reared back. "Just like that?"

Matt recounted Leah's story. "And now, showing up at the school…"

"That's not exactly sinister. If she's on

the level, it'd make sense that she'd want to see where and how he's being educated."

"Or how she can get to him," Matt replied darkly.

"You think she's planning to snatch him?"

"I don't know," he admitted. "It's what I've been asking myself ever since she showed up."

"But then she'd be opening herself up to a legal nightmare." Roger shook his head. "Unless she's completely stupid, that wouldn't make any sense."

"Hmm."

"Have you considered that she could be good for Danny?"

"In what possible way?"

"Every kid wants a mother, Matt. She may not be perfect, but she is his mother."

"Not perfect? What if she gets to know him, gets bored and walks away again? No. I'm not going to let Danny get hurt like that. He deserves the best, and up till now that's what I've tried to give him. She could tear all that down, make him doubt the foundation he's always trusted."

"Are you sure she's really as bad as all that? I mean, you said she just got into town. How do you know what kind of person she is? It's been eight years. She could have changed. Sounds like she was just a kid herself when she had him."

"She's going to say all the right things," Matt protested.

"Have you got a choice? At least here, it's on your turf. If you get into lawyers, she could win. Mothers always have the edge in custody cases, even when they shouldn't. Think about it. What better place is there to learn who the real Leah is?"

Matt didn't want to learn who the real Leah was. He kept picturing his brother when he'd returned home, shaky, almost frightened.

But Roger was right. He had a better chance of uncovering the real Leah here in Rosewood than anywhere else.

Within a few days, Leah had discovered which classroom Danny was in and had met his teacher. One of the younger teachers, Miss Randolph was open and friendly. But then Leah had found that the entire staff was pretty much that way. As part of the Community Church, the school reflected the church's attitude, Annie had explained.

When Leah volunteered to help out in the class, Miss Randolph was happy to have her. Nervous about her first day, Leah brought cupcakes to smooth the way. Annie, now her staunch supporter, had offered both the use of her kitchen and her grandmother's cake recipe. But Leah had painted the faces on the cupcakes herself with layers of multicolored icing. Tigers, lions, giraffes, bears.

Now that the time had come to offer them to the children, Miss Randolph clapped her hands together. "Okay, let's line up for treats."

Accustomed to the routine, the kids got into an orderly line. As prearranged, Leah held the large platter of cupcakes. The kids were used to treats, but eyes widened when they saw the elaborate animal faces with realistic whiskers and expressions.

Pleased, Leah relaxed somewhat. But it was difficult to pull her focus from Danny. She wanted to watch his every move. Knowing she couldn't single out one child for her attention, she tried to be casual, tried not to stare.

But he was so lively. And interested in everything.

All of the children were intrigued by the unusual treats and took care choosing just which animal they wanted. When it was Danny's turn, he scrunched his face into concentrated lines, then picked the lion.

"Thanks," he said politely with an upturned grin. "These are cool."

"You're welcome."

"Did you make 'em?"

"Yes," she replied, wanting to say more, but knowing she couldn't. Especially since she felt the sting of tears. The cupcake was the first thing she'd given him…the first thing he'd been able to thank her for. Such a simple, ordinary occurrence.

And it meant the world.

She kept it together as she handed out

the rest of the treats and then did cleanup duty. But her gaze continued to stray until the teacher divided the children into reading groups. Leah was supposed to help anyone who needed it.

Since the class, like all the others in the school, was small, so were the individual groups. Leah rotated between them as Miss Randolph had instructed, but she was drawn to Danny's.

Danny read his section aloud without error.

It was a little girl named Lily's turn. She was obviously much shyer. "The water hit the wall with a big…" She paused, trying to decipher the word.

"Splash," Danny whispered.

Lily smiled. "Splash," she said aloud, then continued reading.

Leah was pleased to see that he was kind to the children who didn't work at his level. That behavior could come naturally.

Or from what he'd been taught.

She had to acknowledge the truth. Danny's upbringing had been a good one. And that was because of Matt.

Beneath the man's glower and glare, there must be something else. Something that had shaped Danny.

By late evening most of the guests at the bed-and-breakfast were either upstairs in their rooms or relaxing in the main parlor. The spacious old house had a small rear parlor off the kitchen that was Annie's private space, one that she invited Leah to share.

"These old Victorian houses are great," Leah said, relaxing in a bentwood rocking chair.

"Some people are put off because they're too big. I think they're cozy. Especially here by the kitchen."

Leah smiled. "I always thought it would be nice to have a sturdy table right in the middle of the kitchen, the family gathering around for meals."

"That not what you're used to?"

"Oh, my mother likes things more formal, dinner in the dining room, using the china and crystal." Leah shrugged, her eyes softening. "This just seems warmer, homier."

"Do you have a very big family?"

"No. I'm an only child. My parents had me kind of late, when they were in their forties. And when I didn't come along in the expected time line, I think they gave up. So I was a surprise. And by then they were used to giving dinner parties, entertaining clientele."

"Sounds lonely."

"I didn't mean it to. They doted on me. Because they were older, their friends were, too, so I had lots of attention. We traveled, which was great. It's just that, sometimes, I wondered about places, well, like Rosewood. Elegant is beautiful, but I wondered about simpler places where rustic is okay, too." Embarrassed, Leah laughed. "Listen to me."

"I'm enjoying it. I don't have many friends from outside of Rosewood and I know practically nothing about city living."

"How about you? How did you come to be the one who inherited your grandparents' house? No siblings to share it with?"

Annie's dark eyes saddened. "When I was a baby, my parents and older brother and sister were killed in a car accident. I was here with my grandparents."

Horrified, Leah stopped rocking and laid one hand over Annie's. "I'm sorry. I shouldn't have pried."

"It's part of who I am." Annie's face was drawn. "Part of the family curse."

"Curse?"

"I don't know what else to call it. I told you my grandparents' first home burned. Their other child, my mother's only brother, died in the fire."

"That doesn't mean your family's cursed, Annie."

"When I was twenty-one I met…the most wonderful man in the world." Annie's voice thickened. "He wasn't from here. He was a tourist just passing through. But after we met…well, anyway, we fell in love. And we got engaged. The day after, I was waiting for him so we could call his parents. When he didn't show up, I got worried and went over to the hotel. He didn't answer when I knocked on his door. The manager finally got the key, and when he opened the door, David was inside. At first I couldn't understand how he could sleep through both of us banging on the door." Annie paused, remembering. "He had died in the night. His heart. The doctor said he must have had a preexisting condition. He was twenty-five years old. I knew then what the preexisting condition was—my family curse."

"Oh, Annie, no! It was a terrible thing to happen, but it wasn't your fault."

"If he'd just kept driving, hadn't met me—"

"You can't believe that!"

Annie leaned back in her chair. "I keep praying it isn't true. But it isn't safe for anyone to become part of my family. Look what happens."

"So you intend to live alone the rest of your life?"

"No. I turned the bakery into a bed-and-breakfast so I have company." Annie smiled, trying, but still not hiding her pain. "And sometimes, when I'm lucky, guests are as good as family."

"I don't believe in curses, and I've always wanted a sister. So, I'll sign on."

Annie's smile faltered. "Don't even joke."

"I'm not. I took a huge leap of faith by trusting you with the most important secret I have. You proved that was the right thing to do. Let me prove this to you."

"Oh, I don't know, Leah. You haven't lived with this fear."

"I've lived with the fear of thinking I might not find my son alive every day of the last eight years. There isn't a greater fear."

Annie's lips trembled. "I've prayed that this curse isn't real."

Leah held out her hand. "Sisters?"

Annie hesitated, then reached out, as well. "Sisters."

Chapter Six

For the next few weeks, work on the teachers' lounge was progressing to Leah's satisfaction. The walls were freshly painted the color of sunwashed sand, and she'd done the trim in bright, clean white, with sections stained a deep mahogany for contrast. It was a drastic change from the dreary institutional green.

An ugly column stood in the middle of the room, and rather than trying to blend it in, Leah decided to make it a focal point. Using a trompe l'oeil technique, she turned it into a graceful willow tree, with a trunk, branches and leaves that reached around all four sides.

Continuing the theme, she used the same method to paint willow trees that faded in to the corners of the room, as well. The windowless, odd-shaped room was now open and inviting. The teachers were thrilled and there wasn't a stick of furniture inside yet. That required Matt's involvement.

He was the furniture man. She didn't want to delay finishing the job, but she didn't want to speak to him.

Problem.

She'd hoped to tiptoe around him by dealing with Nan at the store. But the older woman had cheerfully offered to have her boss get back to Leah.

Leah had come to the school that morning to complete a few touch-ups. The lounge door was propped open to allow the paint to dry, and she could hear footsteps, sure and distinctive, approaching from down the hall.

Instinctively, Leah knew it was him. She braced herself before facing him.

He wasn't smiling. He never did around her. Not that she expected him to.

For an instant she wondered how it felt to be in his shoes. To have raised Danny, to have had him at his side all this time. To wonder if he would be taken away.

Something in her softened. "Thanks for coming," she said as he walked in to the room

"I was close by. Nan gave me your message." He glanced around. "The place looks a lot different."

"Better, I hope."

He cocked his head, examining the center column. "Yeah."

More pleased than she would have expected, Leah smiled. "I was hoping we could replace the rectangular tables with some round ones, if that's possible. Hopefully in varied sizes."

"The school doesn't keep a huge inventory of furniture in stock."

She pursed her lips. "It's just that a few round tables would be better for the teachers, especially if they need privacy to work on a project. And with the odd angles in this room, well… But I know they like to sit together, too…."

"I can see if we could do some switching around," he said grudgingly. "Maybe with the library—"

"That would be great!"

"I didn't say for sure," he warned her.

"I understand." Leah proffered a sketch pad with a drawing of the room featuring assorted round tables. "I've got some great red chenille that I want to recover the chairs in."

"You don't think that's too ambitious?"

Leah felt a flash of temper. "You're doubting me?"

"It's a lot of work."

"Give me some credit, Matt. I'm a designer. I'm used to hard work. Do you think these walls painted themselves?"

"Give *me* some credit. When you're at your fancy design firm, you're not painting walls and recovering chairs yourself. You have people who do all of that."

"I learned from the ground up. We don't send jobbers out to do anything we don't know how to do ourselves, except electrical and plumbing. Maybe you ought to stop making assumptions and start learning about me, Matt. That's what I decided to do about you. Even if I don't like everything I find out." The last admission cost her, but she didn't back down.

He searched her eyes, then sighed. "Yeah. I can't do less than I expect of Danny."

"What?"

"I just reminded him that the easiest route isn't always the right one."

"Does that mean—"

"No assumptions, that's all, Leah."

It wasn't much. But it was a start.

The Sunday morning service at Rosewood Community Church was packed. Afterward, as the members dispersed, Annie began introducing Leah to some of her friends.

Leah sensed a kindred spirit in Emma McAllister, owner of the local costume shop.

"Welcome to Rosewood. You'll find we're a caring community. I was a stranger a few years back myself." Emma's arm rested on the shoulders of her son, Toby, who held the hand of his younger sister, just a toddler. Her handsome husband, Seth, had been equally friendly. "But it's difficult to stay a stranger long."

"Annie's convinced me of that."

Emma smiled. "Please stop by the shop so we can talk. The kids will keep things lively, but I'd like you to meet my partner, Tina."

Leah was touched by her openness. "That's very kind of you."

"It's not easy to be new, but you couldn't have chosen a better place for it." Toby tugged on her hand. "Now, I'd better catch up with my husband, but I'll be watching for you at the shop, okay?"

"Okay."

Annie nudged her. "I told you not to be nervous about today."

"You were right."

"And there are more people I want you to meet, too." When Leah started to protest, she held up a hand. "Okay. Not all at once."

Leah smiled, then spotted Matt and Danny walking in her direction. They were dressed in matching suits—the tall man, the small boy. Matt held Danny's hand securely in his own. Their bond was deep. So deep.

Danny saw her at about the same time. And smiled.

Her heart melted.

"Dad! It's the cupcake lady!"

Matt didn't have enough warning to avoid her.

"From my school! The animal cupcakes."

Matt cleared his throat. "Danny told me all about the cupcakes. They must have been something."

Impossibly touched, Leah shrugged. "I had fun making them."

"And she doesn't even have a kid in the class," Danny told Matt.

Leah's smile faltered, but she tried to hide the pain.

"Danny said the whiskers looked real," Matt told her in a quiet voice. "He had a hard time deciding between the lion and tiger. He said he picked the lion because the mane was so thick, but he wanted both."

Leah met Matt's eyes, silently thanking him for the time to recover.

"Yeah, I liked all of them!"

"Tell you what. How about if I make you one of each? And you share them with your Dad?"

Danny's eyes widened. "Really? Wow!" Then he glanced up at Matt. "Would that be okay?"

Matt put a hand on Danny's shoulders. "That would be nice of Leah."

Danny grinned. "Are you comin' back to my class?"

"Yes. Would you like that?"

"Uh-huh." Then he frowned. "But you can't give me special cupcakes in front of the other kids. It wouldn't be fair." He brightened. "But you could come to our house." He glanced up again at Matt. "Couldn't she, Dad?"

It was evident he wanted to say no. An emphatic no. "Well—"

"And we could all share the cupcakes!" Danny's excitement grew.

Just what Matt wanted. But Danny was nearly dancing in his freshly shined shoes.

"Leah's probably too busy—"

"No," she replied, unwilling to relinquish any opportunity to spend time with her son. "I have plenty of time. Just tell me when."

Matt edged a step backward. "I'll have to check my calendar."

"There's nothin' on it for Thursday," Danny piped up helpfully. "I know 'cause I filled in the squares for soccer and softball practice nights."

Trapped, Matt forced out the invitation. "So, Thursday?"

"Thursday," she agreed. Cupcakes with her son. It was one of the fantasies she'd dreamed of a thousand times. To share the simple moments.

Try It On design and costume shop was located right in the middle of Main Street. When it opened, it had been a tiny place, and it was during the remodeling that Emma had fallen in love with her contractor, Seth McAllister.

In the witness protection program at the time, she couldn't tell him the truth about herself. It was a situation that didn't change until it was nearly too late.

Emma and Seth had each lost a child. Remarkably, Toby had come into their lives and they were able to adopt him. And now, the Lord had blessed them with another child, Ashley.

As a result, Emma had made her longtime associate and friend, Tina, her business partner. Still single, Tina had more hours to put in than Emma did these days. But Emma had installed a playpen in her office, making the business a family-friendly establishment.

It was crazy at times, especially when they were planning a big event like a wedding. Designs, fabric and people crowded the shop, and keeping an eye on her little one was a challenge. But Emma didn't want to miss a single moment of her daughter's life.

Nor did she want to miss out on new friends, which was why she was glad to see Leah Hunter pausing outside the shop's front door.

"Tina! Company!"

“The woman you told me about?” Tina called out from the back room.

“Yep.”

The bell tinkled over the door as Leah pushed it open.

“Come on in,” Emma invited, walking toward her. “I’m so glad you decided to come by.”

“I hope I didn’t pick a busy time.”

“Not at all. Tina’s just making some tea. Tuesdays are rarely busy, and we just finished one of the biggest weddings we’ve ever done. We’ve had a little breather, but now the elementary school…actually, the one at the community church, is gearing up for a play.”

“And you’re doing costumes as well as wedding parties?” Leah asked, impressed.

Emma grinned. “I love it.”

“I can imagine why. The play must be the most fun. I’m already picturing the kids dressed up—they must look so cute!”

“Especially when they’re little frogs or butterflies or daisies. The more inventive, the better for me.”

Leah leaned over to touch the bolts of

fabric lined up against one wall. "You have some beautiful materials."

"Thanks. I don't know how they look to a real professional."

Leah pulled her mouth down on one side. "You're joking, of course.

"No. This is my second career. My first was the law."

"It certainly doesn't show." Leah walked over to one of the costumes hanging on the wall. "Is this an original design?"

"Yes."

"It's exquisite."

"Thank you," Emma replied.

"I was supposed to make tea," Tina announced, carrying in baby Ashley on her hip. "But someone wasn't asleep."

The child, newly awakened, had that rosy glow only children and pregnant women possessed, one that automatically stirred smiles. Shyly, Ashley laid her face against Tina's shoulder when she spotted Leah.

"Oh, now you don't want to hide," Emma coaxed gently.

"Mama," Ashley replied.

"And Mama's new friend, Leah."

Ashley lifted her head slowly, looking over Leah carefully. When she was satisfied, she wriggled a bit and Tina put her down. She toddled her way over to Leah.

Seeing that she was coming her way, Leah knelt down. "Hey there."

Ashley thrust her plump hands out and Leah caught them.

"What a pretty girl you are," Leah cooed.

"You're a natural with her," Emma said quietly.

Leah tipped her head to one side, smiling at the baby. "She's so sweet."

Emma smiled, too. "I think so. But we're easily charmed."

"True," Tina agreed.

Leah's face had softened. "Oh, I can see why."

Perhaps it was the loss of her own child, or a gift the Lord had bestowed on her because of it, but Emma could now sense a similar loss in others, and she felt it now in Leah Hunter. Emma wondered if that was why He had led Leah to Rosewood.

There was still pain in her eyes. Emma

had seen it when they met on Sunday. Oh, it was carefully hidden. But her own had been, too. Before Seth, before the Lord had helped her through it, had made her whole again.

Watching Leah with her latest blessing, Emma silently promised the Lord she would help Leah as much as everyone in Rosewood had helped her. To be one of the friends she sensed Leah would need.

"I'm so glad I came by today." Leah inhaled the sweet baby fragrance as Ashley allowed a hug. It was as if she couldn't get enough of that precious unmistakable scent.

"Me, too."

"And now I can get that tea," Tina called over her shoulder, heading into the back room.

"Whatever." Leah smiled at Ashley, who smiled back. "I have everything I need right here to entertain me."

Chapter Seven

By Thursday, Matt was examining his sanity. He'd had one weak moment Sunday when Leah had looked so vulnerable and hurt. But to invite her here…

He groaned. History was full of tales of strong men destroyed by allowing their enemies to get too close.

Okay, enemy might be a little harsh. But he and Leah weren't far from that. They both wanted Danny. And only one of them could have him.

He poured cream into his mother's old earthenware pitcher and put it on the table. He'd avoided Leah over the past week, but he'd seen the work she'd done. She'd finished the teachers' lounge. It looked good.

No.

He had to admit it looked great. He wouldn't have believed it could be done. That misshapen room had been an eyesore. Now it was the buzz of the whole school. Of course, most of it was trompe l'oeil. Like Leah, real on the surface, but no substance.

He wasn't sure how the teachers were going to like the round tables she'd cajoled him into giving her. She was good at that. The cajoling. It worried him. Would she be able to sway Danny the same way? First volunteering in the school, now cupcakes...what was next? She had talked his brother into marriage before John was ready. Could she convince Danny he would be happier somewhere else? With her?

Taking the sugar bowl from the cupboard, he plunked it on the table. Of course, she probably used some fake sugar he didn't have. Not that he was running a Starbucks.

She probably thought a hick from Rosewood hadn't even heard of Starbucks. His mother's gentle yet firm voice twigged his conscience, reminding him that a guest should always be treated well.

That shouldn't be a concern. Danny had been running around all afternoon on hyperspeed. He'd insisted on buying ice cream, two flavors, to go with the cupcakes. And he'd volunteered to clean his room, in case Leah wanted to see it.

Matt had never seen him so excited about a guest. And it worried him more than he wanted to admit.

"Dad, do you think I oughta go wait by the mailbox so she won't miss our house?"

"No. She'll find it."

"What time did you tell her to come?"

"Seven o'clock."

"It's almost seven o'clock now. Maybe she's lost."

"Maybe she's almost here," Matt replied patiently. "Put the napkins on the table."

Danny complied, but it only took a few

moments to lay out three napkins. "I could wait on the porch."

Matt mentally counted to three. "If you want to."

Danny was off like a shot, the screen door banging behind him. The wide porch was like another room with its chairs, glider and tables. In the summer they used it as living and dining room. Shaded by tall oak trees, it was quiet and cool. When Matt was a kid, his parents used to crank homemade ice cream here, then spend long evening after the last of it had melted, holding hands even after he had dozed off. He knew because sometimes he would wake briefly to see them sitting with their fingers intertwined, their voices low.

He missed them both. His dad had been gone so long now. Matt had been only six when he died of cancer. And his mother had married John's father a year and a half year later. But Tom Johnson hadn't been the man his mother thought he was. Not bad, just weak. Too weak to give John the grounding he needed.

Matt wondered what his mother would think of the situation now. Of Leah coming back, claiming to want Danny. His mother had been a wise, strong woman. Her one weak decision might have been in choosing her second husband, but Matt knew she'd done it for the right reasons—for him, so they'd have a whole family again, so he wouldn't grow up without a father.

His mother's life had been all about sacrifice. Everything she'd done had been for her sons, her family. And she'd always made him feel that she was exactly where she wanted to be…that he and John were loved, wanted.

One of his biggest regrets was that his mother hadn't lived to know Danny. She would have devoted herself to her grandson just as she had her sons.

And she would have been able to discern the truth about Leah.

He heard the spin of gravel in the driveway, the rush of Danny's feet as he ran to meet her, then the garble of voices, Danny's chatter in a high, excited voice.

As Matt went to join them, he just couldn't get over the way his son had taken to her. Biology, nature, whatever, she was still a stranger.

Leah walked up the path, the late sun striking her long, wavy red-blond hair. Danny's hair was dark like his own, but the shape of their eyes and mouths…those were a match. And when they reached the bottom of the wide steps and looked up at him, more than the shape of their eyes matched. The color, the unusual green that hadn't belonged to anyone in his family, was there in duplicate.

Matt swallowed hard.

"Hey, Dad, it's Leah."

She held up a plastic container. "The cupcake lady."

"Come in. I just made fresh coffee."

"And we have milk," Danny told her. "Sometimes, we even get to have chocolate milk."

Leah smiled. "That sounds good. Guess what? Some of these cupcakes are chocolate."

Danny grinned. "Yay!"

"We eat in the kitchen here, nothing fancy." Matt gestured toward the big table when they reached it. Probably didn't compare with what she was used to in the city.

Leah put the container on the table. "Looks good." She ran her hand over the smooth, sturdy surface. "Is this one of your pieces?"

"One of my first. I made it for my mother...."

She looked as though she wanted to ask about her. "I like how solid it is."

His designs had evolved since those early days. They were more sophisticated, far more developed, but he wasn't ashamed of this table, or anything else in his house. He hadn't given Danny elegance. He'd given him something better, something long lasting.

Leah lifted out the cupcakes, placing them on a large square platter Matt had set out. "I added a dog and cat to the circus animals. Hope you like pets, too."

"Uh-huh." Danny climbed onto one of the chairs. "We had a dog, Roxie, but she died."

"I'm sorry. It's hard to lose someone you love. You must miss her."

"Uh-huh. But she's in heaven now."

Leah's eyes misted. "Then she's happy."

Matt suspected she was just saying what she thought they expected to hear. She had her act down good.

Danny's eyes were roving over the cupcakes. Clearly he was having a hard time trying to decide between them.

"Gentlemen, I'm leaving all the extras here, so don't strain yourselves making your first-round picks."

Her words seemed to make Danny decide, and he chose the puppy.

She'd made long floppy ears on the pup, her favorite, as well.

Matt took two mugs from the cabinet. "Coffee?"

"Please."

Danny reached into the freezer and removed the ice cream, holding up the cartons. "We have chocolate and vanilla."

She smiled. "I like both, so I'll have whatever you're having."

"You get to pick."

He looked so serious Leah suspected this was important. Chin in hand, she concentrated. "If it's okay with your dad, we could have a scoop of each."

"Yay! That's what we get to do on special days."

Relieved that she'd gotten it right, Leah smiled back. "Can I help with the scooping?"

"Okay. Sometimes it gets kind of stuck, you know."

"Absolutely." But that was okay, because it gave her an opportunity to cover his small hand with hers.

Matt glanced at the bowls. "*Small* scoops, Danny."

"Okay, Dad."

She had so much to learn about being a good parent. It *didn't* all come naturally. Left to her own devices, she'd have let him eat too much and he'd probably have ended up with a stomachache.

Subdued, Leah accepted a mug of coffee and watched Danny.

He carefully peeled the wrapper off one

cupcake and took a bite. "Tastes real good."

"I'm glad."

Danny swallowed another bite. "Do you have to cook a lot?"

She tilted her head. "No. I hardly ever cook, actually."

"Is that on account of you don't have a husband?"

Leah almost choked on her coffee. "Uh, no, I don't."

Matt drew his eyebrows together in an admonishing glare, but Danny missed it.

"Or a boyfriend?"

"Danny!"

Leah swallowed the hot liquid in her mouth. "It's okay. No, Danny, I don't have a boyfriend. Why?"

His shoulders bunched upward. "I just wondered."

"I wonder about lots of things, too." She scrunched her eyebrows together. "Tell me about you."

"I got into Scouts this year. You have to be eight."

"That's great."

"Me and Dad go campin' and fishin'. And that's gonna help get me some of my badges." He wriggled in his chair. "And we make furniture. Dad showed me how. I use real tools, not baby ones, but you gotta be careful and use safety goggles and stuff 'cause they're not toys."

"Of course not. Wow, that keeps you pretty busy."

"We play soccer. Dad's the coach. And I play Little League."

They did so much together. "Thank you for having me over tonight. I can tell you don't have much free time."

"It's okay," Danny answered candidly. "I like you."

"I like you, too."

Danny finished his cupcake and ice cream. "You wanna see my room?"

"If it's all right with your dad." She glanced at Matt.

"It's not exactly a highlight on the Rosewood tour…."

"Aw, Dad!"

Matt's designs spoke from every corner of the bedroom. Furniture of soft native pine had been built so there were no square edges. With any other designer the pieces might seem too safe to be creative. But there was creativity in each stroke. Leah recognized the inspiration. It came from carvings made by the Black Forest artisans of the eighteenth century. Matt must have painstakingly formed the thickly roped furniture out of singular pieces of wood. Leah ran her hand over the surface. It was as smooth as fine silk.

"These are my fish," Danny told her proudly, leading her over to a tank at his eye level. "And Dudley, my turtle."

"I had a turtle," she remembered. But she'd wanted a dog. A dog that would shed, her mother had explained regretfully.

"What was your turtle's name?" Danny asked.

"Shelley."

"That sounds like a girl's name."

"I think she was a girl turtle," Leah explained. It wasn't a fact she would have wanted put to the test. They all looked the same to her.

"Oh."

"This is a super room. You know, my job is decorating rooms, and I've never seen a kid's room with furniture this special before."

"Really?"

"Really."

"My dad made it."

"I thought so."

"He can make anything."

She swallowed. *Matt was his hero.* "That's great." *She wouldn't cry.* "Really great."

"Do you like my dad?"

She kept her eyes on Danny, refusing to look at Matt. "Sure."

"Good. 'Cause he's the best dad in the world."

Matt cleared his throat. "I thought you wanted to show Leah around the garden."

"Oh, yeah. Do you like flowers 'n' stuff? We plant stuff every year. I like watermelon best. But Billy—he's my best friend—he likes cantaloupe best. And Dad likes the tomatoes. He says you can smell the sunshine in 'em. We don't plant yucky vegetables like spinach." He made a face. "But Dad puts some of the stuff we grow on the grill and it tastes real good. You wanna come have supper with us and see?"

She darted a glance toward Matt. "That would be nice sometime."

"We don't have a lot of company for dinner 'cept maybe Billy or Roger," Danny continued.

Leah guessed that Matt probably wasn't thrilled with having the details of his life spilled out like the seeds in his garden had been. "Did you help plant everything?" she asked Danny as they headed outside.

"Dad showed me how." They walked beside the neat rows in the vegetable garden, then moved on to the older, mature flower gardens that twined around and beside the house.

"My grandma planted the rose bushes," Danny explained. "When they grow flowers, they'll be yellow."

"Yellow roses of Texas," she murmured.

"My mother's favorite," Matt said quietly.

Hearing the traces of pain that lingered in his voice, she turned to him. "I'm sure they're beautiful."

He reached out, cupping the tender leaves in his hand. "She gave them lots of TLC. Like she did her family. All of us." His gaze challenged her on the issue of Kyle.

But she wouldn't pursue it in front of Danny. "How long has she been gone?"

"She died about ten years ago—heart attack."

Danny looked up at her. "I didn't know my grandma. Dad says I missed a lot."

"I'm sure you did, sweetie."

"I didn't know my mother, either."

Leah caught her breath.

"But I could get a new mother. If my dad gets married."

Chapter Eight

The upcoming play by the elementary grades was the buzz of the entire Community Church and school. The production was a favorite of teachers, parents and the community. Whether the smallest actors remembered their parts was of little consequence when they looked so adorable in their costumes.

Leah offered to help Emma McAllister with the outfits. She and Annie both. It was slow at Borbey House, so the two of them had volunteered to spend the morning at Emma's costume shop.

"I appreciate your help—I can use all the extra hands I can recruit." Emma lifted a bolt of shimmery yellow fabric. "How would this look as an overlay for our littlest ears of corn?"

"Perfect," Leah murmured. The play was about the Lord's bounty. The youngest children were going to portray nature's elements while the major speaking parts would go to kids in the older grades.

Annie picked up a roll of grass-colored fringe. "I heard it's an original play, written by one of the teachers."

"Apparently they've done Noah's Ark to death and they wanted something more meaningful than *Alice in Wonderland.* And the choices narrow when you want enough parts for everyone to participate." Emma shifted the fabric to her cutting table.

"The school's lucky to have a playwright on staff." Leah slid a bit of the material between her thumb and forefinger. "Which teacher is it?"

"Ethan Warren. Wrote it in his spare time. He's single and says he has lots of that available."

Leah glanced meaningfully at Annie, who ignored her with equal resolve. "Is he an old, graying bachelor who's done this all his life?"

Emma laughed. "Early thirties, a thick head of dark hair, not a gray straggler among them. Are you interested?"

"Hmm. I'll have to think about it. I signed up to help build sets, too. Will you be in charge of those?"

Emma shook her head. "This is all I can handle. Matt Whitaker heads that group."

Of course. She should have seen that coming.

Focusing on her work, Emma cut the material in a straight line. "And he doesn't have any gray stragglers that I've noticed, either."

Startled, Leah jerked her head up, her eyes round, her mouth open.

Emma shrugged. "In case you wondered," she added, her tone mild.

Was that an innocent remark? Leah couldn't tell. There was a twinkle in Emma's eyes and she was certain Tina had grinned.

"I have enough chicken salad in the fridge in the back room to make a decent lunch," Tina announced. "I can run across the street and get some croissants, we have tea…"

"If you're waiting for objections, you won't get one from me," Leah told her.

"Me, either," Annie chimed in.

"You know my vote," Emma added. "The baby's asleep in her crib, which won't happen in a restaurant."

"This really is the ideal setup, isn't it?" Leah mused.

"I'm blessed." Emma moved a stack of sketches. "A few years ago I thought I was destined to live out the rest of my life alone. Now I don't take a single day for granted."

"You're wise," Leah said. "Little Ashley will grow up quickly…more quickly than you can imagine." She paused. "Let me go to the bakery and pick up the croissants."

"And I can pop home and pick up a fresh pie for dessert," Annie suggested.

Tina rubbed her hands together. "This meal is really shaping up."

* * *

A light breeze skipped leaves across the sidewalk and tossed them into the street.

Leah dug in her purse for her wallet. "Ethan Warren sounds like just the perk you deserve for volunteering to help on this project."

"Thanks for not blurting that out in front of Emma and Tina."

"I sensed that. Annie, remember you agreed we'd take on this curse thing together."

Annie shook her head. "But Ethan Warren didn't volunteer to be a guinea pig."

"Do you hear yourself? Did you volunteer to lose your family members? Of course not. And I didn't volunteer to lose Danny when he was a baby. But we can't just stand back and accept it, Annie. We're sisters now, remember? And I don't give up on family."

"I don't know…."

"It'll only sting a little at first. You'll see."

"Sounds like an inoculation."

Smiling, Leah shrugged. "I *could* say something cheesy like you get a passport to romance with these inoculations…."

Annie groaned.

"I said I *could* say it…."

"Tell me this was the part that stings."

"Okay, right." Leah laughed. "Definitely the part that stings."

Set building brought out hammers, wood, paint and more opinions than a school play warranted. Being the new kid on the block, Leah decided she probably ought to keep hers to herself.

But when she saw *nature* being portrayed in colors nature didn't possess, she was hard-pressed to keep silent.

Several helpful parents had donated leftover cans of paint. She wondered why so many of them owned lime, orange, pink and lemon, all in neon, but it was pointed out that they were extremely popular colors with the kids. Leah flipped open her cell phone, made an urgent call to L.A., checked the warehouse, found there was plenty of paint in the overrun materials section in more natural colors and arranged to have it shipped.

"We're not used to high-powered intervention," Matt told her, obviously having overheard the conversation.

Crestfallen, she stared at him. "Having seen your work, I'd have thought you'd want nature to look more, well...natural. Besides, it's not high-powered. These are overrun materials. Paint that sits too long gets thick, then gets thrown away. Why not use it here?"

"That's not the point. This is a production the parents, children and teachers put on."

Chastised, Leah felt once again the outsider. "I was only trying to help. Can't the neon paints be used for other projects?"

"I don't know. But you can't ship all the materials for the sets from L.A. The parents look forward to this. It's something they want to be part of, and for some of them, especially ones without a lot of money, that means donating the props. And they won't be perfect. This is *Rosewood.* Simple, uncomplicated, no frills Rosewood."

"Then *Nature's Bounty* shouldn't be

neon," she retorted, keeping her voice quiet so none of the parents would overhear.

"Is this how you plan to fit in? By turning Rosewood into a mini L.A.?"

"Hardly," she muttered.

"John said you and your family had to have everything your way."

"Which gave him carte blanche to steal my child, I suppose!"

"So you admit it?"

"I admit no such thing. Just because I had a good idea—"

"Problem?" Ethan asked, coming up behind them.

Leah cringed, then turned to the writer/director of the play. "Apparently I overstepped my bounds when I sent for some paint that's not in the neon palette."

"Do we have to pay for it?"

"No."

"Good deal!" Ethan grinned. "We don't have enough money in the budget for all we need, and I wasn't sure I could talk the hardware store into donating that many gallons. Neon lime grass wasn't quite the look I imagined for the play."

Leah met Matt's cryptic gaze. "My thoughts exactly. Mr. Whitaker was concerned that the parents who donated the paints would be offended if they aren't used. I thought they could be used for other projects."

Ethan nodded. "Or we can use them for the signs to advertise the play. The kids are going to make those in art class."

"What a *great* idea!" Leah laid it on so thick, it was a wonder her voice didn't clog.

"I'm excited to have a volunteer with your enthusiasm," Ethan assured her. "Feel free to share your ideas. Even though we want to consider the parents' feelings, we can always use some new blood to stir things up."

She smiled. "I'll keep that in mind."

"Mr. Warren!" A harried teacher approached, gripping a stack of scripts.

"Duty calls. Thanks for getting the paint, Mrs.—"

"Miss. Hunter. Leah. And you're welcome." He was nice. And if he was unattached, he might be just right for Annie.

She broadened her smile, but it disappeared as she turned to Matt. He looked even sterner than usual. "What now?"

"Nothing."

"You mentioned props. With this nature theme, are you going to be building a lot of them?"

"Probably."

"I haven't seen any sketches, but I can make the padded scenery."

Matt stared at her, then reluctantly opened a slim leather portfolio. "These are still kind of rough."

But his talent was obvious. The same talent that she'd seen in the extraordinary pieces of furniture he designed, even the small box that had brought her to Rosewood. But he hadn't made these too complicated. The sets were simple enough to showcase the children. "They're good."

He glanced at her. "You wouldn't change anything?"

"No. And even though you don't want to hear it, they deserve better than neon paint."

"You're worse than a dog with a bone."

"That's a flattering picture." To fill the

awkward moment, she studied the designs again. "Have you thought about using real wheat for motion and dimension?"

"No."

"Maybe some potted field grass and thistle? Wouldn't cost anything. I've seen the thistle growing wild here in the ditches. And, if they wanted to, those parents you mentioned who help with props could pick some."

"Danny has a speaking part."

Scenery forgotten, she stared at him. "I thought only the older kids did."

"It's only one line actually."

"Still..." Ridiculously touched and proud, Leah grinned. "He'll be the best one in the whole play."

Matt seemed to forget their animosity for a moment. "Yeah. He will."

Annie's clogs clacked as she approached. "Leah!" Her voice rose on the second syllable, causing it to sound like an accusation. Both Leah and Matt turned to her.

Annie pointed at Leah. "I need to talk to you." Taking her arm, Annie dragged

Leah away. "How could you? We've barely started working on the play, and now Ethan thinks I'm after him. This is too humiliating. I'll have to quit. And it's not as though Rosewood's big enough to lose myself in. Why couldn't you leave it alone and—"

"Hold it! I haven't done anything."

"Right. He just started talking to me for no reason."

Leah smiled gently at her new friend, noticing the pretty blouse she'd worn, the extra care she'd taken with her makeup, the earrings that brought out the dark glow of her eyes, her softly brushed hair. "He had plenty of reason. Take a look in the mirror."

Annie narrowed disbelieving eyes. "You really didn't say anything?"

"Cross my heart." Leah clapped her hands. "But I couldn't have planned it better if I *had* intervened. He seems really nice, don't you think? And he goes to your church, all information courtesy of Emma. And married women are the best source."

Annie's pretty face paled. "How do I tell him he's going to be a guinea pig?"

"Oh, Annie! Do you really think you're meant to be alone?"

Her friend's mouth opened, then closed.

"I don't think so, either. Even better, it looks as though Ethan Warren's a *very* smart man."

Chapter Nine

The following week, the set builders and the costume crew shared the auditorium. As Matt worked, he could watch the comings and goings.

Parents had warmed to Leah's suggestions for gathering thistles and other wild grasses that grew in the ditch banks and fields, free for the taking.

It was that knack of hers, he realized, for drawing people in, convincing them of her ideas. The same quality that worried him when it came to Danny. She'd already ingratiated herself with the teachers in the school. How could an eight-year-old resist such strong appeal?

Danny talked about her all the time, the *cupcake* lady. How she could draw and paint, how she was the best volunteer his class had *ever* had. How nice she was. How her treats were the kids' favorites.

Matt couldn't tell Danny that it was probably all an act. Or at best, a temporary situation. That Leah would soon get tired of baking treats and volunteering in an elementary school.

He doubted he could convince any of the parents, either. She was winning them over, as well.

Roger handed him a sheet of plywood. "You look like you've been chewing on rusty nails."

Matt grunted. "Just thinking."

"Then think about something more cheerful." He shrugged. "Picture the kids when this is done. Danny's told me his line at least a hundred times already. The kid's so hyped, you'd think he was starring in his own Disney flick." Roger glanced across the auditorium at Leah, who was waist deep in piles of fabric. "You've been awfully quiet about her. Is that because she's changed?"

"Changed?"

"Volunteering, making costumes. Danny says she brought over cupcakes."

"Danny sounds like the Rosewood grapevine. He tell you anything else?"

"Touchy, touchy. Anything else to tell?"

"No. Just that she's making sure she's part of everything, so I can't keep her away from Danny."

Roger pushed his cap back and scratched his head. "Let me see if I've got this straight. You were afraid that she was just here for a little while till she got bored. Now you're afraid she's making herself a part of everything, which means she could be around for a good while."

"I thought you were here to help, not talk."

Roger reached for a clamp. "Yeah, yeah."

Leah climbed the wide, shallow steps that curved around the stage. She smiled at Roger, then held out some soft white fabric for Matt to examine. "How do you like this for padding the clouds? It's not a pure white, so I think it looks more realistic. What do you think?"

"It's fine," he muttered.

"Try to hold down your enthusiasm."

Roger chuckled.

She grinned at him. "I'm Leah Hunter."

"Roger O'Brien. Good to meet you. And I think the fabric looks like a cloud should."

"Thanks. I know it's not Broadway, but…"

"It's for the kids and that's what counts."

"Exactly. I want it to be perfect." She held up the fabric. "I'd better get back to work."

"Sure." Roger waited until she was out of earshot. "I wouldn't mind having her stick around."

Matt grunted.

"You still have that thorn in your paw? She's nice, and in case something's wrong with your eyesight, she's also pretty. Wouldn't be a hardship for me to be around her."

"Just like that?"

Roger thumped the side of his head with his middle finger. "*If* she treats Danny right, of course. But I wouldn't be setting up the roadblocks you are."

His friend had always seen the easier side of life, Matt thought. He hadn't heard all the terrible things Leah had said about his brother, things Matt knew couldn't be true.

Although she was worming her way into the community, it didn't mean she intended to stick around. It could be her way of making him relax his guard. Even now she could have attorneys preparing papers to back up her threats.

And he wasn't blind, either. He'd noticed how pretty she was.

But he *was* scared.

She was insinuating herself into every aspect of Danny's life that she could. Danny had just told him that she was one of the volunteers for tomorrow's field trip to the zoo in San Antonio. Danny wanted to sit beside her on the bus, and also at lunch.

Matt felt as though he was fighting to keep his son's attention. And he couldn't compete with her flashy projects. His was a steadier attention, one that didn't impress little boys.

* * *

The clouds darkened briefly in the dawn sky, but as the bus rolled toward San Antonio, the weather cleared. The kids, primed for a day in the city, sang and cheered as they drove first on the small farm-to-market roads, then reached the main highway.

Danny got his wish and sat next to Leah. Although there were plenty of chaperones for the group of eight to ten year olds, they were still far outnumbered by the kids.

Matt sat across the aisle from Danny and Leah. As she leaned forward in her seat, Leah's long, strawberry-blond hair was ruffled by the breeze. The wind didn't seem to bother her as she sang along with the kids, laughing aloud at the silly hand movements, then clapping in unison with Danny.

Usually the bus ride seemed to be the longest part of these field trips for Matt, but he was so absorbed by his son's interaction with Leah, he was startled when he realized they were already in San Antonio, pulling up in front of the zoo.

As soon as they got off the bus, the kids

started calling out their favorite animals: elephants, monkeys, tigers, lions. Miss Randolph had their route already planned out, including breaks and lunch.

"I love the giraffes," Leah confided as she and Danny migrated next to him. "I hope they're on the list."

Giraffes were an unusual favorite. "Any special reason?"

"They're so gentle. And how can anyone resist their huge eyes with those incredible lashes?"

He looked into her unusual eyes as she glanced up at him. And he saw something different. Something that had nothing to do with his son. Nothing to do with their differences.

"We're starting with Amazonia," Miss Randolph told the children. "What do we know about this part of the zoo?"

The kids jumped up and down. "Those are animals that live in the Amazon!"

"Guess that leaves out the giraffes," Leah murmured. Then she smiled. "But I bet we make it to Africa."

"And the aquarium," Danny told her.

"That's what I wanna see. Zillions of fish, and this zoo's 'posed to have 'em all."

One of the largest in the country, the San Antonio zoo had more than thirty-five hundred animals—seven hundred and fifty species, from white and black rhino to snow leopard to whooping cranes. The premier facility also put conservation at the top of its priorities, along with educating children.

As they left Amazonia and strolled to the African plains, they saw many of the kids' favorites: elephants, zebras and, as they neared the valley that led to the treetop lookouts, the giraffes.

"Ooh!" Leah squealed, sounding as young as Danny. A family of giraffes moved gracefully together, their long legs taller than the trunks of the nearby trees. Close up, their strength was evident in their thick limbs and muscled bodies.

Both the mother and father kept their large eyes trained on the youngster. Not typical in the animal kingdom, Matt thought. But they were an unusual species.

It was time to take a break. Even though

the kids claimed they could keep going, eager to see the lions and then head on to the Australian Walkabout, they were happy with their cold drinks and burgers.

"We're gonna see the aquarium, aren't we, Leah?" Danny asked as he finished his burger.

"Sure! I got to see my giraffes, didn't I?"

"I think the bird house is after the walk-about, pal," Matt told him. "There's a lot to see here in one day."

"But Leah said we'd get to see the aquarium!"

Matt cleared his throat. "We'll try to fit everything in, but Miss Randolph has a tight schedule to keep. All the kids have special things they want to see and we have to be fair."

Danny kicked the concrete table.

"Don't we?" Matt insisted.

"I still wanna see the aquarium."

Leah looked pleadingly at Matt. "Maybe there'll be enough time."

But there were a lot of exhibits left on Miss Randolph's schedule. And the teachers wanted to get back to Rosewood before nightfall. Neither Matt nor the bus driver had liked the look of the skies that morning. As beautiful as the hill country was, its weather could be equally treacherous, especially in March.

"Danny, we have to stick to Miss Randolph's schedule, do you understand?"

Danny stared at the table, then nodded. "Yes, sir."

"So, no unplanned trips to the aquarium."

"Yes, sir."

As Danny ran to join Billy and some other friends, Leah tried to lighten the mood. "At least he's not obsessed with the snake house." She shuddered. "I'm with Danny on this one. I'd rather look at fish, too."

"If all of the kids demanded their own agenda, think of the mess we'd have."

"Well, yes, but—"

"It's not always easy to say no, but sometimes it's necessary."

Leah frowned. "And there's no room to be flexible?"

"I know the routine. This isn't my first field trip."

Her lips thinned and he saw the pleasure she'd been having dim. "But it's mine. Thanks for the reminder."

Didn't she see they had to set the boundaries? That they had to be the *parents?* At least he did. He could have explained, but what was the point? This was just a temporary gig for her.

Refreshed by the break, the kids were excited to see the Australian animals. By the time they'd visited the wetlands exhibit, they were running behind schedule and the weather was shifting. The snake house was still left to see, but Matt recommended skipping it.

As he conferred with Miss Randolph, she was at first reluctant, then agreed.

They stopped at the restrooms for the last time before heading home, then made their way back to the bus for a head count. Two short. It took Matt only a few moments to realize Danny and Leah were the ones missing.

Matt and a couple other parents agreed to search for them. The other two started with the restrooms. Matt glanced toward the aquarium. No. Danny wouldn't disobey a direct order. Instead, backtracking to the last exhibit, Matt searched the area, but they weren't anywhere in sight. Danny had said something about wanting an ice cream, but they weren't in the snack area, either.

Matt checked his watch. He'd already wasted nearly an hour. He flipped open his cell phone, wishing he had Leah's number. He hadn't thought to get it. But then the chaperones weren't supposed to wander away. He'd gotten numbers for the other searchers and called them, but they hadn't found Leah and Danny yet. They agreed to look in the snake house.

Danny had grumbled about passing by the water fowl too quickly, but they weren't there when Matt looked, nor were they in the bird house.

The aquarium.

Leah wouldn't have ignored his instructions.... Making his way over there, Matt felt a mix of disbelief, anger and relief when he spotted Danny inside, standing next to Leah as they ogled the fish. He could have appreciated the fascinating display of underwater creatures if he hadn't wanted to choke both of them.

Fighting to control his anger, Matt phoned the other chaperones and called off the search. He stalked up behind the two of them. Oblivious to his presence, they continued to stare at the display.

He latched one firm hand on Danny's shoulder.

The boy turned around, his expression suddenly guilty. "Dad."

Leah turned, too. "Matt! Did you decide to come and see the aquarium, too?"

"No. I've been searching the grounds for you and Danny."

She glanced at her watch. "Oh! I guess we've been in here longer than I realized."

"That's not the point. We came here as a group. Everyone else is waiting for you on the bus."

Danny hung his head.

Leah rushed to explain. "I thought we could come in here while everyone else was in the snake house since Danny wanted so badly to see the aquarium."

"We skipped the snake house because the weather's turning. Now we've wasted more than an hour searching for you two."

"I didn't think it would hurt anything," Leah tried to explain.

"You didn't *think.*" Matt glanced down at Danny, who avoided his eyes. "And, Danny, who knows better, went along with you. Talking him into disobeying *does* hurt."

She swallowed. "Matt, I—"

"Let's get going.

The mood was tense as they made their way to the bus and headed home. The sky was now muddy gray and deep navy, streaked with bright flashes of lightning.

The bolder children saw the coming storm as an adventure. The more timid ones curled up on the bench seats of the bus, some with quivering lips, some holding hands, many wanting their mothers.

Leah's guilt was immense. While she'd been in the warm, comfortable aquarium, the storm had been gathering. And although the number of chaperones had seemed adequate during the day, now there seemed too few to comfort the scared children. What had she been thinking? She'd only wanted to please Danny. It had seemed like such a small thing at the time. But she hadn't thought through the consequences.

Danny was visibly miserable. Disappointing Matt, upsetting his friends and teacher hadn't been worth the side trip to the aquarium. As the adult, she should have known that.

The rain began before they left San Antonio, slowing the traffic down even more.

By the time they reached the highway, the rain sluiced over the bus in drenching sheets.

Even though it was a few hours before nightfall, darkness had already descended, stealing the last of the daylight. The children, dressed in T-shirts and shorts, shivered in the cooler temperatures. Fortunately, they'd all been instructed to bring outerwear.

Leah, along with the other chaperones, bundled the kids into their jackets. There were a few blankets in the first-aid kit, but not nearly enough to go around. She used her own jacket to spread over the legs of two little girls who were shivering.

If the group hadn't been delayed by her actions, they'd nearly be in Rosewood by now, instead of just leaving San Antonio. Leah gulped as she thought of what lay ahead—dusty, steep-shouldered washes that could fill with water and overflow.

This was so much worse than giving a child a stomachache. Had missing all the years since Danny's birth blunted her intuition about children? Stolen her instincts?

She wondered how the driver could even see through the thick rain and murky gloom. There were no streetlights on the highway as they left the city, and the situation was even worse when they turned off onto the smaller roads.

Matt stayed in the front of the bus, helping the driver by watching road markings and signs.

Leah, who was circulating among the children, slipped in place beside Danny. He still looked miserable.

"Are you scared?" she asked.

He shook his head.

"Danny, I want to apologize. Your dad was right. I wasn't thinking when I suggested going to the aquarium. I honestly didn't think I was causing you to disobey your…dad, but in retrospect… I mean, now that I've thought about it, that's exactly what I did. Which was wrong. And I'm sorry. I would never purposely want you to disobey him or cause you to break your promise."

Danny thought about her words for a minute. "It's okay. I shoulda said no."

Oh, he was a good kid. "You're letting me off easy. I *am* the grown-up. I should have known better."

"My dad taught me to do the right thing." Danny shrugged. "So I shoulda known, too."

She wanted to hug him to pieces. She settled for ruffling his hair. "You warm enough?"

"Yeah. I'm not a *girl*."

She bit back her smile. "What was I thinking?"

Feeling somewhat relieved, Leah settled back in the seat and stared out the rain-streaked windows. There was nothing to see but darkness, though. Not much traffic was on the road, just the occasional flash of headlights. Matt and the driver had the radio turned on the weather station, but they kept the volume low. Leah wondered if there were any flood warnings in place. The other chaperones occasionally walked up to the front of the bus, spoke with Matt and returned to their seats, looking tense and worried.

Leah didn't want to worry Danny, and she guessed he would be too curious to be put off with a vague answer, so she didn't go check the radio.

As they bumped along, Leah thought about her next apology, guessing it wouldn't be as easy, or as easily accepted.

The unexpected light from flashing strobes atop emergency vehicles split the night. Everyone on the bus leaned toward the windows, peering outside. The bus slowed, then stopped. The driver opened the door. Immediately, the fierce rain pelted inside as a highway patrolman entered, his rain gear dripping puddles on the steps.

"Bridge ahead is near washout," he told them. "Road's closed."

"How long?" the driver asked.

"Don't know. At least till morning. Flood warning's in place until six a.m. Best to get turned around. I'm not sure how stable this road is. It could wash out, too."

"Thanks, officer."

"Be careful, folks. There's enough room to get the bus turned around—just barely, without getting it stuck. I'll watch for you out here, signal with my flashlight if you get too close to the drop-off."

"Thanks."

A flash of lightning lit the bus and Leah caught Matt glancing back at her. She could read the blame in it all the way from where she sat.

It was tight turning around on the two-lane road. And as the driver retraced their route, there was nowhere close and dry to wait out the storm.

Miss Randolph motioned from the front

of the bus for all the chaperones to come speak to her. "We're going to have to try to contact the parents. I don't know what kind of signals we'll get out here—we may be out of range, and what with the storm...but we need to try. If you get through to *anyone,* have them contact Principal Gunderland. She'll have a list of the kids who are on the bus and she can start a phoning relay."

"What do we tell them?" Leah asked. "About where we're going to stay tonight?"

"That's a tough one. We don't know yet. Just that we'll find someplace dry and safe. Emphasize that the kids are all right."

Leah looked at the circle of worried faces. "I'm sorry that I delayed our return. If Danny and I had been back on the bus—"

Miss Randolph clasped her hand. "Don't give that another thought. The storm would have happened regardless."

Leah avoided looking at Matt.

"Now," the teacher continued, "we have to call on our strengths. Let's pray." She bowed her head. "Lord, please be with us, guard us and watch over us, help us to be strong for these precious children in our care, keep us always mindful that we are in Your sight and in Your hands. Amen."

Feeling calmer, Leah walked back and took her seat beside Danny.

"What's going on?"

"We're going back the way we came until we find a place to spend the night."

"Like a motel?"

"I guess so." Leah couldn't remember passing one in quite some time. The logistics of bedding down this many children was boggling. They'd need a dormitory to do it properly.

But first she needed to follow Miss Randolph's instructions and try her cell phone. The one number she called frequently in Rosewood was Annie. She turned on her cell but there wasn't any signal. Not surprising. They were in the middle of nowhere surrounded by a lashing storm that sounded like it was peeling the paint off the bus.

The rain pelted down even harder as they drove into the darkness. There was a lonely feel to driving in the night away from home, toward the unknown.

It seemed they drove along the deserted road for miles and miles. Locals, listening to weather reports and their own good sense, were probably secure in their homes.

At last the bus approached a bypass just off the main highway. The driver turned in at the only building they'd seen, a large truck stop. The covered parking lot was filled with eighteen-wheelers whose drivers had hunkered down to ride out the storm.

Miss Randolph consulted with Matt and the bus driver, then motioned to her volunteers. "Looks like we can park here for the night," she said when they gathered around her.

So much for my notion of a motel, Leah thought.

"Mr. Whitaker's going to check on hot meals."

"I'd like to pay for those," Leah offered. She met Matt's gaze. "On my credit card—it'll be the easiest way."

"That's very generous," Miss Randolph said. "We'll sort it out when we get back and repay you from school funds. I'm going inside with Mr. Whitaker to check on the phone."

The kids watched out the windows, silent, until Matt and their teacher reappeared.

"Looks like they can handle us," Matt said. "Plenty of empty booths and tables."

After phoning the principal, Miss Randolph and the chaperones lined the kids up and took them inside. The storm didn't seem as scary once they'd had a warm meal, milk and hot peach cobbler.

As the children finished eating, Leah searched the aisles of the shop in the truck stop, collecting all the souvenir T-shirts the store had in children's and adult sizes, along with jackets and ballcaps. She found some soft stadium seats emblazoned with "San Antonio Spurs" that could be used for pillows.

Returning to the group, she told Miss Randolph about her purchase. Delighted, the teacher asked a few other chaperones to help her carry the bounty to the bus. "Don't forget to save the receipt so we can reimburse you, Leah. We can pass out the T-shirts and jackets and see how far they'll stretch. Already an answer to prayer."

Leah and another mother cut off tags, then sorted the clothing. The other parents watched the kids as they stretched their legs in the store and used the restrooms.

By the time they were ready to board the bus, word of their situation had gotten around to the truckers. As the children climbed back onto the bus and received a T-shirt or jacket, drivers of the big rigs started bringing them blankets. Most said they were extras, all insisted on donating them for the kids.

Between the T-shirts, jackets and blankets, all the kids were warmly covered as they settled in for the night.

Danny still insisted that Leah sit beside him. Matt didn't want to make a scene, but he was deeply disappointed in his son's behavior. It wasn't like Danny to bend under a bad influence. But Leah was an adult, which was a completely new experience. The adults in his life, up until now, had provided good role models.

Since he and the bus driver were the only men on the trip, Matt kept watch so the others could sleep. They should be safe, parked in the truck stop, but the bus had no locks on its doors.

Tired after the long day, the children quickly succumbed to sleep, many of them slumped against one another. Even Miss Randolph and the chaperones gave in to their exhaustion.

As the soft sounds of slumber filled the bus, Matt moved down the center aisle to check on Danny. He had fallen asleep, stretched out on Leah's lap. To his surprise, she was still awake.

"I thought everyone was asleep."

She shook her head. "I keep thinking about what I did today, how wrong it was…in so many ways." She bit her lip. "I've apologized to Danny. But there hasn't been an opportunity to apologize to you. I'm so sorry. You were right. I *didn't* think. I not only did something wrong, I caused Danny to do something wrong, something he knew was wrong."

"You don't have to—"

"It didn't seem such a big thing at the time. I just thought if everyone else was going to the snake house, it wouldn't hurt if we went to the aquarium. The truth is, I wanted to give him something he wanted. I hated to see him disappointed. And look what happened. I caused Danny to break his word to you. I stranded an entire busload of children. No credit card is going to fix this, is it? All the parents are going to be worried sick until they see their children tomorrow. I've disrupted all those families." She leaned her head back against the seat, and he could see the trembling in her throat. Her eyelids flickered rapidly as she clamped down hard on her lip and he realized she was trying not to cry.

"What you did was wrong. There's no two ways about it."

She nodded.

"But if you're smart, you'll learn from today."

Leah glanced down at Danny. "There's one thing you'll never have to doubt—how much I love him, how I would never hurt him. No matter how many years or miles separated us, he has always been in my heart. Like you, I would die for him." She stroked the hair on Danny's forehead, her touch gentle. "Children are so vulnerable. I used to think about all the things I would do with him when I found him… ironically, the zoo was on my list. But I didn't dwell on the challenge of teaching him the lessons of life, the important things. The things you've been teaching him. He feels terrible, you know, about disappointing you. Which means you've done all that part right."

Matt was silent. He couldn't imagine the last eight years of his life without his son, especially after having held Danny in his arms the first time. To have had him taken away…

But then he pictured his younger brother. For all his reckless impatience, there wasn't that kind of evil or anger in him. John wouldn't have stolen his own child from its mother. He just wouldn't.

And the way she'd acted today...reckless, immature. It was all she'd accused John of being. How could he begin to know what to believe?

Chapter Ten

By morning the storm had passed and the road had held. Water had poured past the banks of the gullies and over the bridge during the night. But now, by midmorning, it was draining down the washes, a benign reminder of what could have been killer flash floods.

After a hearty breakfast, the chaperones assisted the children back onto the bus for the return journey to Rosewood. As soon as the bus pulled up in front of the school, Leah could hear the cheers go up from the group of anxious parents gathered there.

The kids cheered back, pounding their tennis shoes against the floor of the bus, and the minute the driver opened the door, they all piled out in a rush.

Miss Randolph made a token effort at order, but it was hopeless.

Leah smiled as she watched the children and parents hug one another. There was an awful lot of happiness in Rosewood that morning. Matt stood with his hands on Danny's shoulders.

Leah tried not to feel as though she was the only singleton on the ark. Parents shook her hands and thanked her, as they did the other chaperones. Leah couldn't help thinking they wouldn't be so grateful if they knew she was the one who'd caused them to be stranded overnight.

Miss Randolph kindly thanked her for volunteering, as though she'd done nothing wrong. Suddenly exhausted and feeling terribly lonely, Leah walked away from the noisy crowd, unwilling to stand there until she was left completely alone.

"Dad?"

"Yes, son?"

"I'm sorry. About goin' to the aquarium."

"I know."

"Leah said it was her fault, but I knew better."

Matt digested this information. "Yes, you did."

Danny kicked at the loose gravel by the curb. "I wanted to see that aquarium awful bad."

"Was it worth all the trouble you caused and the way you've felt since?"

"No." They walked almost the length of the block before Danny spoke again. "Dad?"

"Yes?"

"How come Leah didn't know that? She's a grown-up."

Matt battled with his conscience. What he said would influence how Danny felt about his mother. But she was no role model. "Grown-ups make mistakes, too."

"That's what she said. She said it was wrong for her to make me make 'em, too."

Matt sighed. In some ways, it seemed as though Leah was beating herself up enough about the incident.

"Do you still like her, Dad?"

Oh, the brutal honesty of children. "Do you?"

"Yeah. Jesus doesn't stop lovin' us when we do somethin' wrong."

No, He doesn't.

"Right, Dad?"

Matt pulled Danny into a hug. "Very right."

Annie brought in a tray with a teapot and cups. "This is a local chamomile blend. Guaranteed to put some color back in your face."

"I'm fine," Leah insisted, glad to be back at the bed-and-breakfast with her *sister,* but still feeling the exhaustion of the entire ordeal.

"Hmm." Annie poured the tea and handed her a cup. "That's why you're so pale, you look like you've been dusted in flour."

Leah grimaced. "A baker's joke?"

"Drink your tea."

She smiled half-heartedly. "You're a bossy landlady."

"I feel responsible, suggesting you make a good impression on the town."

"Don't." Leah took a sip of the soothing tea.

Annie offered a plate of small, plain cookies. "They're kind of like ginger-snaps. They'll settle your stomach."

"My stomach's fine," Leah insisted, but she gratefully took a cookie.

Annie poured a cup of tea for herself and took a gingersnap. "I'm not sure mine is."

"I really let Danny down. I always thought that given a chance I'd be a great mother, and instead…"

"Give yourself a break. For eight years you've wanted to do things for Danny. No wonder the dam burst. I think you should get an award for your restraint up until now."

"Not if Matt Whitaker's on the awards committee."

"Even he's got to see that you didn't plan what happened. Besides, the important thing to remember is everything worked out okay. The children are all fine, including Danny. And, as you work on the school play together, he'll get to know you, see what kind of person you are."

Leah groaned. She'd forgotten about the play. And facing Matt.

Ethan Warren had a way with the kids. They listened to his direction. The older ones came to rehearsal early and stayed late. The younger ones gained a sense of confidence on the stage, little ears of corn mingling with farmers and fishermen.

Danny was excited by every rehearsal, reciting his single line to anyone who would listen.

Matt grinned, watching him. He glanced toward the volunteers rushing around backstage. Leah was fitting costumes amid the madness, but she looked unperturbed.

The sets were nearly finished. Roger had helped him with all the large pieces. Except for some touch-ups, the only pieces left to be mounted were the clouds. He'd expected Leah to be right in the middle of set construction, but she'd distanced herself. In the week since the field trip she'd been making costumes. And quietly encouraging Danny. But she'd avoided him.

So, had she folded under the first bit of

pressure as a parent? And did that mean she was about to run again? If so, he needed to know, before Danny became too attached. Picking up one of the cloud cutouts, he crossed the space between them.

Leah kept her attention on the pair of overalls she was adjusting. “Hi.”

“Are you going to have time to work on these clouds,” he asked, “or should I plan on padding them?”

“Oh.” Her expression skipped from looking trapped to guilty. “I’ll do them. I have all the materials.”

“Ethan wants everything in place for the dress rehearsal. If you’re behind, I can take care of them.”

She stuck a pin in the pin cushion. “I said I’ll do them.”

“Costumes coming along okay?”

“Yes. I’m just helping. Emma’s in charge of them. Her store looks like Santa’s workshop.”

He leaned against the doorjamb. “You say that as though it’s a given Santa’s workshop exists.”

She sighed.

"And that you've seen it."

She glanced up, a smile reluctantly edging the corners of her mouth. "Yeah. It's one of my regular stops every Christmas."

"You really *do* have connections then."

That made her laugh. "I try not to brag."

"I won't spread it around." He shifted the wood cutouts in his hands. "You really plan on sticking around until the play opens?"

Her smile dissolved. "What's that supposed to mean?"

"If you're planning to take off, I'd like to know. It'll give me time to come up with a plausible story for Danny."

She stiffened. "Your family's real good at making up stories, but it won't be necessary. This time you're not dealing with a teenager. And trust me, there's not a place on the planet you can hide Danny. Not this time."

By the evening of the play, not only the children were brimming with excitement. The community gave its usual support, filling the auditorium, along with parents and families of the junior thespians.

Principal Gunderland welcomed everyone to the *worldwide* debut of Ethan Warren's original play, *Nature's Bounty.*

Everyone oohed and aahed as the youngest members of the cast, dressed in Emma's imaginative costumes as seeds, grain, ears of corns, leaves, birds and butterflies, filled the stage. Then the older actors, portraying farmers, dairy processors and ranchers, joined them.

Leah held her breath as the play progressed and the time came for Danny's part. He was one of the leaves. Their costumes were green in the front, with yellow sides and reddish orange backs.

Matt was situated off to one side of the stage. Shortly after Danny's line he would have to change the scenery. But instinctively, despite the anger she was still nursing toward him, Leah knew he must be on pins and needles, too.

Then it was time for Danny's line. Confident and sure, he spoke in a clear, high voice. "When I change color, it's time for fall!"

In unison, all the green leaves turned around, revealing their reddish orange backs. The audience, delighted, broke into applause.

Smiling widely, Leah looked across the stage, meeting Matt's gaze. For that single instant they shared the parental bond of sheer pride. Of joy in their child's accomplishment.

Then it was time for Matt to shift the backdrop. Leah's heart beat faster. In pride, she told herself. Just pride.

After the play was over, Leah was still smiling. It was another milestone for her. So many memories in such a short time; she felt she was making a scrapbook in her heart.

Milling around the auditorium with other parents, she started toward the exit, when Danny ran up to her, tugging her hand.

"Leah, wait!"

"Hey, there," she greeted him. "Great job, Danny! You were the best leaf in the play!"

"Thanks! You wanna come get ice cream with us?"

Matt was a few feet behind Danny and she glanced at him to see if he was in agreement.

He looked uncomfortable.

But Danny wasn't to be stopped. "We're going to the drugstore on Main Street. They make the best ice cream in the world!"

"This side of the Mississippi," Matt corrected.

"And the fountain is made of marbles."

"Really?"

"It's one of the oldest marble ice-cream fountains left in the country," Matt muttered.

"How can I resist? Especially with such a handsome young man for an escort?"

Danny giggled.

"I haven't had a banana split in...well, so long I can't remember when," Leah mused. "So, does this ice-cream *fountain* have banana splits?"

"Sure. Haven't you been to an ice-cream fountain before?"

Matt smothered an unexpected laugh with a cough.

"Yes, but not the best one this side of

the Mississippi. You'll have to show me what's what."

"They have booths, but we sit at the counter," Danny told her.

She nodded, realizing this was important information.

"That way you get to see 'em make everything. And sometimes they give you extra cherries, especially if Clyde's working."

Obviously, *very* important information.

"But you're not supposed to ask for them," he continued.

"I see."

"It's not polite." He was so serious she wanted to smile, but she didn't.

"I understand."

"Did you drive?" Matt asked.

She shook her head. "No. I rode over with Emma, but I told her I'd walk home."

"Then you can come with us," Danny invited. "We got lots of room."

Lots was relative, Leah realized, as she sat next to Matt in the pickup truck. Danny, using the manners Matt had taught him, insisted that she get in first.

She'd known Matt was tall, but sitting

beside him, her shoulder wedged against him, she realized that hers only came to the middle of his arm.

As he shifted the gears, she could see the easy play of his muscles. He was a man who worked with his hands, and she'd been aware that he was strong and fit. But somehow it hadn't hit her with the punch that it did now.

Swallowing, she tried to sit still and straight, not to take more than her allotted space, or sway when the truck turned. She didn't need this complication. This unwanted, unwarranted attraction to her son's father. A man who was more irritating than a scratchy wool sweater in the dead of summer.

Still, she was almost painfully aware of him as they drove to the drugstore. While nothing was far in Rosewood, the blocks seemed like miles.

Other families had had the same idea and the drugstore was crowded. The booths filled fast but there were three empty stools at the counter. The old-fashioned soda fountain was wide and deep, a thick slab of marble covering the counter. Tall, long handled levers dispensed soda, and deep refrigerated wells held the ice cream. An incredible assortment of sauces, sprinkles, candies, nuts and sliced fruit was lined up along the back of the counter, with an array of specially shaped dishes and glasses.

"I get to order whatever I want," Danny told her.

"That's because you're a star."

He laughed. "Nuh-uh."

"Ask your dad."

"You were great, pal."

Danny grinned. "Billy said I'd forget what to say."

"But you didn't," Leah and Matt replied in unison. Surprised that they had, their voices trailed off.

"Jinx," Danny announced. Then he lowered his voice to a whisper. "I hope I get extra cherries."

Leah couldn't contain her grin. "Me, too."

They watched with fascination as the young man making the sodas for other customers "jerked" the levers with precise movements so the glasses were filled just to the top and didn't overflow. Danny told Leah he wanted to be a soda jerk, too, when he was older. Leah guessed that Rosewood might be one of the few places left in the country with the kind of soda fountain that would need one.

The banana split was loaded with everything wonderful, but it wasn't the foot-long, foot-high variety that novelty ice-cream stores in the cities had begun serving. Leah wasn't certain who those appealed to—possibly small nations or large families, but certainly not single women. But this, this was a real banana split. Warm, homemade hot fudge bathed the smooth ice cream and melted it just enough to drown the bananas. Yum.

Matt dipped into his own ice cream. "From the look on your face, I'd say you like it."

"I can't believe I've been staying only a block away from this place and haven't tried the ice cream."

"I'd eat ice cream here every day if I

lived on Main Street," Danny said between bites.

Their server had placed four extra cherries on Danny's double caramel and hot fudge sundae. "I can see why. They obviously like you here."

"They know I like cherries," Danny confided.

She looked at him with such longing she felt her heart expanding even more. Oh, this child of hers. Yes, hers. How could anyone not want to spoil him?

"We've been coming here since Danny was a toddler," Matt explained. "They know him pretty well."

"One of the advantages of a small town," she acknowledged.

"Yes."

"Big cities have stuff we don't." Danny plucked one of the cherries from his sundae.

"I come from a big city, you know. Los Angeles."

"Do you like it?"

"Yes."

"Do you like it better'n Rosewood?"

She hesitated. "Not better, just different."

"How's it different?" He scooped up a spoonful of ice cream drenched in hot fudge.

She thought for a moment. "Like you said, big cities have things small towns don't, like museums."

"We have a museum. It's gotta two-headed calf and a civil war uniform in it."

Matt met her gaze. His seemed to say *top that.*

"There are different kinds of museums. We have the Getty with all kinds of wonderful paintings and sculptures."

"Oh."

"And the Huntington. It has real Japanese gardens."

"Uh-huh." He swallowed his ice cream.

Sensing she was drowning fast, she grasped for a lifeline. "And museums of natural science with dinosaurs."

"Dinosaurs are cool," Danny replied. "The museum in Houston has this really huge dinosaur that goes all the way to the roof."

And Houston was in reasonable driving distance from Rosewood.

Was that a smirk she saw on Matt's face? She wanted to tell him not to gloat yet. She'd barely begun on the advantages L.A. could offer. But tonight wasn't the time to list them. Not when they were having such a good time in one of Danny's favorite places in Rosewood.

However, she would begin. Because Rosewood didn't have the one crucial thing Danny did need. A mother.

Chapter Eleven

Warm currents of air carried the scent of freshly cut wood from Matt's shop. Sawdust littered the floor, the shavings curling beneath their feet.

"Hey, Dad."

"Son."

"I been thinkin'."

"Anything special?"

"Kinda."

Matt put down the sander and waited.

"You know how Billy's gonna have a new brother or sister?"

Matt nodded.

"Well, I was thinkin'. Maybe we could

make it a cradle. People give the new baby presents, don't they?"

Matt knew how hard it was for Danny to accept that Billy would have a new sibling when there wasn't one on the horizon for him. "Yes, son, they do. And I think a cradle would be a fine present. We could start on it this afternoon, if you'd like."

"Yeah. That'd be good."

They picked out the wood, settling on a native pine. And for a while they worked on the cradle's design in relative quiet.

But Matt couldn't contain his pleasure at Danny's gesture. "It's tough, Billy getting a new brother or sister when you're not, and I'm proud of you for being a good friend."

"It's okay. Besides, I'm prayin'."

"We've discussed this. First I have to meet someone and get married—"

"I know, Dad, that's what I'm prayin' for. That you'll have somebody to love. So we can have a brother or sister like Billy."

Matt swallowed. He couldn't honestly tell Danny his prayer was wrong.

"You should have somebody else to love besides me 'cause I'll grow up," Danny continued earnestly. "And the other grown-ups all have somebody."

Matt's heart caught.

"Like the other kids have mothers," Danny continued.

There it was. The bittersweet truth he couldn't pretend didn't exist.

"Do you miss having a mother?"

Danny shrugged. Then he kicked his tennis shoe against the toeboard beneath the main workbench. "Billy's mom's nice. And she smells good."

Of course he missed having a mother. Matt remembered how important his own mother had been to him, how she'd nursed him through his illnesses and childhood wounds, both physical and emotional. His father had been a strong and wonderful presence in his life but his mother had provided the tenderness. He'd thought he could do it all…but obviously he couldn't.

He thought of his daily prayers, asking the Lord to let him keep Danny. Swallowing, he realized he should have been asking Him to do what was best for his son. Even if that meant letting him go.

* * *

Annie had polished the parlor furniture until the old rosewood pieces shone as brightly as the waxed floors. The scent of lemon oil and beeswax pervaded the entire bed-and-breakfast, blending with the aromas of today's pies—blackberry and apple crumb.

She'd been up since dawn, cleaning the life out of the already immaculate house. Now she was carefully removing each crystal teardrop from the elaborate chandelier in the dining room, wiping them individually.

"I didn't know we were having the president for dinner," Leah mused, watching her friend.

Annie flushed. "The school's artistic committee is holding their meeting here tonight."

"Oh. Ooh…! Isn't that Ethan Warren's committee?"

"Yes, I believe it is." Annie tried to look nonchalant. She failed miserably.

"Why didn't you tell me? What do you want me to do? Not that the house doesn't already look spotless. But I can clean. And cook. You need to primp for tonight, not work on the house." Leah reached for one of Annie's hands. "You've ruined your manicure doing all this cleaning. First, we have to do your nails. Can we get you in somewhere today? And is the place in town good? If not, I can do a decent manicure. And your hair, hmm..."

Annie's hands flew to her hair. "What's wrong with my hair?"

"Nothing. Just, how do you plan to wear it tonight?"

"I haven't given it any thought."

Leah took the dust cloth out of Annie's hands. "Okay. You're through. *I'm* in charge of cleaning from this minute on. *You're* in charge of looking gorgeous. I bet you haven't even decided what to wear."

"I'm not sure...."

"Have you thought about something new?"

Annie shook her head.

"Think about it. Also, you can borrow anything of mine you want. You like that melon outfit. And it would look great with your coloring."

"I wouldn't feel right—"

"Hey, we're sisters, remember? From what I've heard, that's what sisters do. Now, scoot. Start the beauty regime while I finish here."

Annie looked both terrified and thrilled. "You're sure?"

"Absolutely."

Annie hugged her, then ran up the stairs.

Leah picked up one of the crystal teardrops, then glanced at the chandelier, trying to figure out just how it was supposed to be attached. "Oh, you and I are *not* going to be friends," she muttered.

By that night, Annie had primped until there was nothing left to primp. Her hands, given over to the care of Rosewood's capable manicurist, were soft and her nails elegant. After she'd darted into her favorite clothes shop and found nothing she liked, she'd agreed to borrow Leah's melon dress, which not only set off her dark hair and eyes, but also brought a certain degree of sophistication that updated her look.

Leah refused to let Annie in the kitchen, and finished the appetizers and pasta salads that her friend had already started. She'd also taken care of any last-minute tidying, and managed to wheedle the reason the committee meeting was being held at Borbey House out of Annie.

"I volunteered," she confessed. "Ethan was saying something about how there never seemed to be enough meeting rooms at the school for all the committees, so I said, why not use the B and B. We usually have an empty spot."

"Good for you!"

"It's a small committee, and apparently there was room on it for at least another person. And it doesn't have to be a teacher...."

"You!" Leah was so pleased for her friend.

Annie bit down on her lower lip. "You really think so? All I've done is volunteer to help for the one play."

Leah smiled knowingly. "Annie, do you

think Ethan would have agreed to hold the meeting here tonight if he weren't interested in you?"

"I'm nervous and scared and excited and, and..."

"Those are good things, you know."

"But what if he really did just want a quiet meeting room?"

"Doesn't the public library have those?"

Annie's big doelike eyes considered this. "I suppose. But they don't allow food in their meeting rooms."

Delighted by her friend's total lack of artifice, Leah laughed. "That's it. He's smitten by your food."

Annie laughed, too. "Well, this is hardly a date. Remember the committee?"

"Sometimes the path to love has company. I'll serve though, so you can hostess."

"This seems all backward," Annie worried. "You're a paying guest and here you're doing all this work—"

"We're sisters, Annie. That's what sisters do, right?"

Annie nodded, her smile suddenly wobbly.

"Don't you dare," Leah warned, struck by what a good friend Annie had become. "You'll ruin your makeup."

The bell over the front door jingled.

"That must be them. Go, go!" Leah urged, feeling more like a mother hen than a friend or sister.

Annie was back in the kitchen within a short time. "Leah, Matt's here."

"Um." Leah looked at the egg salad she still had to assemble. "Ask him to come in here, I guess."

"I can take over."

"Oh, no, you can't."

She had her hands in the mixing bowl when Matt appeared. He seemed startled to see her covered by a baker's apron. "Come on in. I can't really stop what I'm doing."

"Will you be done soon?"

"With this? Yes. Then I'll stuff it in the minicroissants. Why?"

"I need to talk to you."

She paused, hearing the serious note in his voice. "Is something wrong? Is Danny okay?"

"Danny's fine."

Her heartbeat settled back down.

"But I do need to talk to you."

She glanced pointedly at the food on the counters. "Actually we've got something special going on tonight. Ethan Warren's coming here and I'm pretty committed to—"

"Can we talk afterward?"

"Well...okay. And you're sure Danny's all right?"

"Yes. He's fine."

Matt left as abruptly as he'd arrived, but Leah didn't have time to worry about him. The bell jangled again, signaling the arrival of Ethan and the rest of the committee. Annie's nerves went into overdrive.

But Leah was used to entertaining. It had been such a part of her life since she was a toddler, and she tried to let her calm confidence rub off on Annie. After awhile, when it was clear that the roof wasn't going to fall in, Annie began to relax.

It was immediately evident to Leah that Ethan Warren hadn't come knocking on

Borbey House's door solely for a convenient meeting place. He watched Annie's smile and delighted in her laughter. And by the end of the evening, she was voted to fill the vacant spot on his committee. Since Annie wasn't a particularly artistic person, that said it all. Leah had done so much talking, she'd gotten herself on the committee, too.

Ethan was the last member to leave the B and B, lingering until the table was cleared and until Leah discreetly withdrew to the kitchen.

It seemed he'd barely had time to drive away when the bell over the door jangled again.

"I don't recall being this busy since the train derailed and I had people sleeping in the halls," Annie declared.

Matt entered the front door.

Spotting him, Leah thumped her forehead. "I completely forgot. I'm so sorry. But we really just finished the meeting."

"That's okay. Do you have some time now?"

"Sure." She glanced around. "Do you

want to sit outside?" Although the B and B fronted Main Street, the wraparound porch led into the backyard, a surprisingly private place. A glider provided a quiet retreat for a talk.

Once they were seated, Leah took a few deep breaths, falling into the calmer rhythm of the night. "I've been running all day. It's good to be still."

"Yes."

When Matt fell silent again, Leah realized he must have something serious to tell her. There was no point putting it off. She needed to know. "You might as well spill it."

"I never filed any legal papers for Danny."

His admission stunned her.

"I never thought I had any need to. I was sure you weren't ever going to come around. I was John's next of kin, his only family."

"So…" she ventured unsurely. "Is this your notice that you're planning to now?"

He sighed, a deep sound from a big man. "No. I've been thinking about what you said…that Los Angeles has a lot to offer that Rosewood doesn't. I know it's more than just museums with dinosaurs. It's a whole life that I can't begin to offer him."

"Are...are you—" she stuttered, unable to form the words.

"Danny wants a mother. You're his mother."

"But...what made you change your mind?"

"I've been thinking about what a strong woman my mother was. She would have given up any and everything for us. And I've been thinking about what you said—that you'd give your life for Danny. Only his mother would do that."

The sudden knot in her throat made it difficult to swallow. "But you said it would be cruel to take Danny away from everything he loves."

Matt bent his head, his voice raw. "I've prayed for an answer, Leah. Don't make me regret telling you the truth."

"And you got this...this answer?"

There was such pain in his eyes, it tore at her to witness it. "Yes."

"You have that much faith?"

"It's how I've always lived my life… how I've raised Danny. It's what I have to put my trust in now."

Chapter Twelve

Songbirds chirped outside her bedroom window, but they didn't waken Leah. She'd been fighting her sheets and light coverlet all night. Giving up the battle for sleep with the birdsong, she padded to the closet and pulled out a T-shirt and cotton pants. She dressed quickly, slipping into her tennis shoes in case her wandering took her farther than she planned.

Freshly baked cinnamon rolls and yeasty bread sent out signals from the bakery that she wasn't the only early riser. But most of the other businesses she passed were closed, and thankfully, no traffic disturbed the silence of the sleepy lanes and shaded neighborhoods.

Leaving Main Street, Leah walked briskly for several blocks until she left the business district behind.

She hoped the morning air would clear her head, bring some sense to her muddled thoughts. Instead she felt the weight of Matt's words as solidly as she had through the night.

Danny wants a mother. You're his mother.

Matt Whitaker hadn't struck her as someone who would have given up easily. But he was a man of truth. And one of faith. And he was laying out both for her to see.

She could take Danny and run to L.A. as fast as she could. Legally, she had the right. Morally…morally she should feel vindicated. Instead, just the thought left a bad taste in her mouth. She'd feel like a thief in the night. This was what she'd come for, what she'd hoped would happen after more time had passed, after she'd convinced Matt what a wonderful mother she was.

What a joke. With her instincts, it was a wonder she didn't need a keeper of her own. Clearly she needed a strong parenting partner like...well, Matt. Someone who instinctively knew the right path for Danny, who made good decisions, and who could help shape and guide him.

Yet Matt had prayed, and based on the answer he felt he'd received, he was willing to trust her with the child he loved with all his heart. Humbled, she wondered what it must be like to have such faith. For all that she had prayed for Danny's return, she'd never had Matt's sure, unwavering belief.

Slowing her pace, measuring her breath, Leah passed beneath century-old magnolias, equally ancient hickory trees, thinking about the solidity of this town. Annie had told her about its history. The settlement was established in the mid 1800s, and neighbor had helped neighbor ever since. Being off the beaten track had not led to the town's demise but had strengthened its sense of community. In a shifting world where she, like most people she knew, found little to depend on, the people of Rosewood had come to depend on each other.

Leah had already met many members of

the Community Church and felt their welcome, their kindness. It spilled over into the school, into social events. And into everything Danny had ever known.

Not that L.A. didn't offer things that Rosewood couldn't. Grandparents for a start. But an entire community of support? A community that embraced the values that had shaped Danny into the loving child he was?

It was truth time now. She was alone with just the sky and the sleeping town.

No. A life in L.A. wasn't the same as growing up in this community. Her own upbringing was evidence.

So. What was the answer? She looked heavenward. She hadn't prayed so much as pleaded with God all those years Danny had been missing. Perhaps she had to learn now how to listen.

The waiting was interminable. A week had passed and Matt hated going to the mailbox, expecting to withdraw an envelope from some fancy L.A. law firm. He hadn't told Leah to pursue the legal options open to them, but he'd given her the go-ahead.

With each phone call, each ring of the doorbell, his blood stilled, then his heart raced. And he questioned his sanity, his good sense, everything but the Lord.

Because the answer had come clear in the still and quiet. He'd given the problem over to Him and He'd answered. And although Matt felt anguished, his heart broken, he couldn't disobey.

Leah must have changed, Matt realized. While he still didn't believe that John had done anything evil, Leah must have changed. The Lord alone would know what was in her heart.

But how to tell Danny?

Of course, he would be excited to have a mother since he wanted one so badly. Matt flipped the calendar pages on the refrigerator. He would complete the cradle they'd started for Billy's new baby brother or sister. Maybe he and Danny could work on it that afternoon. It was Saturday and they didn't have anything planned.

The doorbell rang.

And his bad feeling returned.

He opened the door. Leah stood there, looking expectant. "Hello."

"Morning," she greeted him.

He took a deep breath. He hadn't really thought out the details, but then maybe that was why she was here, to iron them out. "Come in."

"Actually, I was wondering if you could come out. You and Danny that is. Just as far as my car."

"Danny's in his room. Just a minute." He went back inside, calling up the stairs. "Danny! Come on down. Leah's here."

It didn't take long for Danny's running footsteps to sound on the wooden stairs.

"Hey!" Danny greeted her.

"Hey yourself! I've got a surprise."

Matt's stomach had sunk so far it was hovering near his knees.

"Neat!" Danny exclaimed.

They followed her to her car. Leah opened the passenger door and lifted out a cardboard box.

Danny's eyes grew round as something in it wriggled.

Kneeling, Leah lowered the box to Danny's level. A golden retriever puppy immediately tried to climb into his arms.

"A puppy!" Danny shouted.

"A puppy," Matt echoed in disbelief.

"A puppy," Leah agreed, grinning. "Since yours died."

The silky-haired pup licked Danny's face.

"Is it really for me?" Danny asked.

"Yes," Leah replied. "That is, if your dad agrees."

Three heads turned in Matt's direction, the puppy seeming to guess his was the vote that counted. It occurred to Matt that he should say something about a puppy being a huge decision, one that should be discussed first. But wasn't there a much larger decision looming on the horizon, one that took all precedence? "Sure."

"Yay!" Danny and Leah chorused.

Danny threw his arms around Leah's neck and hugged her. She held on, obviously cherishing this first hug.

"Thanks, Leah."

"You're welcome, sweetie."

He turned back to the puppy, who latched on and started chewing on his ear. Laughing, Danny carried the dog to the grass beneath the oak tree where they could play.

Her hand shaky, Leah took a paper from her pocket. "He's already started his puppy shots—they're all written down here. But he has to have more in four weeks."

"Just like a baby." Matt couldn't stop the response.

Her expression was soft. "Pretty much. But then you've been through the long nights, the getting into everything stage."

From a distance, Danny and the puppy rolled in the grass, Danny's giggles drifting in the morning air.

Matt took her hand, surprising both of them. "Why? Unless..."

"No. The puppy means I think Danny's where he belongs. But, Matt... It doesn't mean I'm ready to let go of him. You were right. I'm his mother. And I want him to know that. When it's time. When he's ready."

Matt felt the peace in his heart that had eluded him since he'd had the answer to his prayer.

He still held Leah's hand. "I'm not sure what to say."

"I guess we have to figure out where to go from here."

He looked at her hand just as she did. Releasing his hold, he stepped back a fraction. Just as quickly she pulled her hand back. This was a truce for Danny's sake, not theirs.

The church social was one of those cake and homemade ice cream affairs that brought out everyone from babies to grandparents, especially since all the women tried to outdo each other with the cakes they brought. Not that anyone ever dared voice that aspect of the tradition. But the two-layer cakes grew to three and then were topped one year by a four-layer. After that, there was no stopping the ladies.

It was the one time of year Annie bypassed her pie-baking skills and poured all her energy into a German chocolate torte that was so rich she suspected it could set off a sugar coma.

Leah wasn't concerned about impressing other women with her domestic skills, but she did have one particular eight-year-old in mind. While Annie slaved over her secret family recipe, Leah kept her butter cake batter simple. But the shape was challenging. A puppy. A fat, rollicking-looking retriever puppy. It took her a while to shape the cake, but it was worth every moment. Frosting and decorating it was relatively easy. Her only moment of panic came when she arrived at the church hall. What if someone cut into the cake before Danny saw it?

But luck was with her. Danny was trailing his father, talking with his friends when she arrived.

"Hey, Leah!" he hollered.

Matt turned at the sound of Danny's voice.

Leah held out the cake a bit self-consciously. "Hi!"

"Cool!" Danny and Billy said together, skidding toward her.

"Jinx!"

"Did you *make* that?" Danny asked in awe.

"Yes," Matt repeated, arriving a few moments behind them. "Did you?"

"Guilty."

"Looks just like Hunter, huh, Dad?"

"Yes, it does."

"Hunter?" Leah echoed.

Matt cleared his throat. "Danny decided to name him after you."

Touched, she nearly wobbled the cake.

Matt reached out and steadied the plate. "Would you like some help carrying that?"

"Thanks." She relinquished it to him.

"Can we go on ahead and see the rest of the cakes, Dad?"

"Okay."

The kids scooted around the slower moving adults, anxious to see the display of mouth-watering goodies.

"He usually comes home from this ready to burst," Matt told her.

She frowned. "What do you do about that?"

"Resign myself to it."

She blinked. "Oh."

"Not everything's black and white. Some gray days we all overindulge."

"This parenting thing is a lot harder than movies and sitcoms would have a person believe."

"It doesn't come with a how-to manual."

"The most important job in the world—it should."

They made their way toward the cake tables, Matt keeping a strong grip on his cargo. "You have to trust your instincts."

She groaned. "I was afraid you were going to say that."

Matt found space on one of the tables for Leah's dog-shaped cake. It was unique among the towering displays of elaborate confections. Self-conscious, Leah was aware of a few speculative glances toward her creation.

"I think you may have started something," Matt murmured.

"As long as Danny likes it."

The men had cranked the tubs of homemade ice cream and many were as proud of their creations as their wives were of their cakes. Peach was a perennial favorite, but Leah was drawn to a vanilla that had been made with real vanilla bean.

"I guess I'm just a plain Jane, but this one gets my vote," she declared, enthralled with the creamy treat.

"Plain Jane?" Matt shook his head. "I don't think so."

Never shy, Leah found herself suddenly possessing two heads with at least as many tongues. Shuffling her feet—did she really only have two?—she struggled to balance her purse and the ice cream, hoping she didn't stumble into Matt. Good grief, what was wrong with her? All he'd said, basically, was that she wasn't ugly as a post.

Deciding to take refuge in the ice cream, she gobbled it down too quickly. The frozen treat hit her head like the proverbial brick, and she tried to pretend it hadn't just made the headache worse.

"Would you like some punch?" Matt asked.

Was that sympathy in his voice? "That would be nice."

He'd barely stepped away when she put

down her ice-cream dish and pressed her hand to her forehead.

She felt someone tugging on her hand. "Leah? You okay?"

"Danny!" She opened her eyes. "Yes. My head hurts, that's all."

He put his small hand on her forehead, looking intent. Absorbed by the gesture, by his matching green eyes and face so close to hers, she simply watched.

After awhile he removed his hand. "You don't have a fever."

"Actually, my head doesn't hurt anymore."

He drew his brows together. "Really?"

"Really." And it was true.

When he smiled, she started to reach out, to hug him. But she stopped as he said, "Hey, Dad. Leah's head hurt, but she doesn't have a fever."

"That's good."

"Yeah."

Leah accepted the cup of punch Matt offered. "Thanks."

"Me and Billy counted. There's more chocolate'n anything else. Mrs. Carruthers put Snickers bars on hers."

"Pace yourself, pal."

"Okay, Dad." And he was off, running to catch up with Billy.

A small handful of musicians were playing old tunes while the crowd milled, breaking into smaller groups, laughing and socializing. There was an awkward silence between the two.

Matt finally cleared his throat. "Veterans of this social. Like I told Danny, you have to pace yourself. Only amateurs try to take it all in at once."

She took a sip of her punch, then smiled.

"What?"

"Just thinking. This is kind of like my old school days. The parties. Only better, you know. Not all that worry and tension."

"What did you worry about?"

Her nerves returned in force. "You know…well, I guess you don't. You were a boy." She took a deep breath. "Worrying about ending up alone. Nobody to talk to."

He stared at her as though in disbelief.

Now thoroughly uncomfortable, she looked off in the opposite direction, toward the exit doors.

"I find it difficult to believe you could ever end up alone, Leah."

"I didn't mean..."

"Not tonight, anyway. I'm not going anywhere.... I mean, if that's all right with you...?"

She was wrong. This didn't remind her of a school party. Those naive days when she'd thought flash was attractive in a guy, which was why John had won her heart.

This was...different. She felt secure beside Matt. And aware. Aware that he was more than Danny's dad.

What did he see when he looked at her? Danny's mother? The woman who'd run out on the most important person in his life?

The music swirled around them, rising up to the rafters of the old church hall. Standing together in the middle of the crowd, Leah tried to hold back her shifting feelings. But the gate had already been unlatched.

Chapter Thirteen

Matt sat in the back room of the store that also served as his office. With all the turmoil in his personal life, he'd gotten behind on his paperwork. Although Nan helped with the books, the correspondence was his responsibility.

A discreet ivory, linen-weave envelope caught his attention. It was the sort of stationery he'd expected when he thought Leah would confirm her intentions to take Danny to L.A.

With a caution he wasn't certain he understood, Matt slit open the envelope. The engraved letterhead was impressive. And as he read, he learned the offer was, too.

Barrington Industries was proposing a buyout of Whitaker Woods. His designs, actually. Their plan was to merchandise his pieces all over the country in their high-end furniture stores.

He was amazed.

Granted, Whitaker Woods had been written up in the *Houston Chronicle* and featured on morning shows in Dallas, Austin and San Antonio, as well. And people had been coming from all parts of the country to buy Matt's furniture. But he'd never imagined an offer of this scope. Barrington… How had they come across him?

His eyes strayed to the return address.

Los Angeles.

Coincidence?

Leah's family probably had considerable influence. Their design firm was a big deal in L.A. Had they brokered a deal with Barrington so that he would have a reason to relocate? Not that the letter specifically mentioned relocation, but it seemed probable.

He thought of Leah's wide smile when

she presented the puppy and told him that Danny was where he should be.

He thought of holding her hand at the ice-cream social. The reaction she'd stirred. Then he thought of what he'd known all along, what John had told him about her.

As he laid the letter down on the desk, a card slid from the envelope.

Leonard Jenkins, Vice President, Acquisitions. Handwritten on the card was a simple note: *We can discuss options in person. Call me to set up a meeting at your office.*

Matt was unfamiliar with the ways of big business, but he was pretty sure that it should be the other way around, that he should have to hoof it to L.A. if he wanted this deal. He believed in his own talent, but he knew he wasn't the only furniture designer in the country. Barrington could afford to sit in L.A., send out their letters and wait for designers to come running.

Disappointment churned in waves of such proportion he felt flattened. For himself. For Danny. Because despite everything, part of him wanted to believe in her.

To believe his son had a good mother, who would love him as much as Matt did. Not one who used deceit to get what she wanted.

But he'd been directed in prayer about his decision. And that he didn't question. But how did he reconcile that with what he'd just learned? He had no choice but to wait and see when she would reveal her plans.

The unmatched smell of freshly carved wood drifted together with that of lemon oil and beeswax. He couldn't imagine leaving all that was familiar. Rosewood was more than just a town. It was roots, church, friends, neighbors, support.

But Danny was his son. And if leaving Rosewood was what it took to be near him, he would do it. Still, the disappointment was bitter as he thought of Leah.

The Scout spaghetti dinner was a big fund-raiser for the troop. The proceeds went to buy new camping equipment. Danny was going to be one of the many Scouts who helped serve the garlic bread, punch and plates of spaghetti.

Leah had bought tickets for herself,

Annie and, so as not to be obvious, the four other members of the school's artistic committee. At only five dollars a ticket it was a bargain to set up her friend with a really nice guy. Shamelessly, she suggested that Ethan meet Annie and her at the B and B so the singles could ride together. The other committee members were married and Leah hoped to meet up with them at the church hall where the dinner was being held.

Again she fussed over Annie, this time pulling out all the clothes she'd packed, along with the last box she'd had her assistant send. She was rapidly filling her room in the bed-and-breakfast. This wasn't the first shipment from her apartment. The antique chifforobe was stuffed, as were the bureau and vanity table. Leah knew she couldn't continue living in one room indefinitely, but there was comfort in the old Victorian home, in having Annie just down the hall. And in not having to make a long-term decision.

Her parents had been pressing her more and more in phone conversations about what she was going to do. She hadn't gotten up the courage to tell them that Danny would be staying in Rosewood. She knew how disappointed they would be. And since she hadn't figured out just what she would do yet, she couldn't see upsetting them. She wanted to be close to Danny. That she was sure of. When she'd first come to Rosewood, she couldn't have imagined giving up her life and career in L.A., but now... Fortunately, she had her trust fund, which would allow her to live in Rosewood indefinitely if she chose to.

But could she and Matt coexist as parents when...well, when she didn't see him as just Danny's father anymore?

A lot of people she knew co-parented from opposite ends of the country. There were holidays, summer vacations. Danny could be in Rosewood the bulk of the time and she could have him those other times.

Leah swallowed hard. That wasn't what she wanted. It wasn't what she wanted for Danny. She thought of what Matt had said about his mother. Sacrifice. She'd sacrificed everything for her sons.

Crushing a linen skirt in her hands, Leah wondered what she was willing to sacrifice for Danny. It wasn't a popular concept these days, giving up everything, especially a career like hers, for family. But did that compare to the sacrifice of a child being shuttled across the country? Not every single parent had a choice. She did. When it was the right time to let Danny know who she was, she could tell him that she would be staying right here in Rosewood.

She relaxed her hands. When would it be the right time to tell him, she wondered? Would he be glad? Had he imagined a certain kind of mother? She thought of Emma McAllister and her effortless mothering techniques. Maybe that was the kind of mom Danny had dreamed of. Sighing, she knew she wasn't anything like Emma.

"Leah?" Annie called from the stairs.

Releasing the now mangled skirt, Leah stood. "Yes?"

"A box just came for you."

"Great!" It was the other box she'd asked

Jennifer to send. She scrambled down the stairs. "Annie, help me get this open."

"What is it?"

"I went shopping just before I left L.A. This stuff was still in the bags."

"Oh, Leah! You don't mean…"

"What are sisters for? You can go shopping via UPS."

"But you haven't even worn the things yourself!"

Leah shrugged. "So? Now let's get this open." Tackling the box with a letter opener from the antique breakfront, she slit open the tape.

As Leah pulled out the first garment, Annie gasped. "I love the color."

The cut and material of the dress were simple, perfect for the evening, and Leah held it up to Annie. "I think it loves you, too." A deep topaz, the dress would look beautiful with Annie's dark hair and eyes. "I hate to say it, but we might have hit gold with the first one out of the box."

They combed through everything else, but the prize was right on top. After several reassurances that it was really all right to wear the brand-new dress, Annie clutched it close, ran upstairs and changed.

Leah gathered the remainder of the clothes and took them to her room. In the box was a blouse that she'd bought because it was the same hue as her eyes. Wistfully, she held it up to her chest and peered in the mirror. But who would be there to notice?

Telling herself not to be a big baby, she clipped the tags from the blouse. There. She would wear it for herself, and because it was a special occasion for Danny.

In minutes she was dressed. She slipped on a pair of delicate gold filigree earrings that dangled from her earlobes to swing lightly beside her long, slender neck. A quick glance in the mirror told her the blouse, paired with a slender skirt and sandals, was perfect.

Leah noticed that Ethan's eyes nearly popped out when he saw Annie. Pleased and feeling very much the mother hen, she managed to scramble into the backseat of the car before Annie could so that the pair could sit together on the drive to the church.

After presenting their tickets at the door,

the maître d', known to them as Billy's dad, checked the seating chart for three available seats. The Scouts had set up the long banquet tables end to end, filling the room. Since most of the town usually turned out for the annual event, the Scouts had come up with the seating plan so they could accommodate as many people at one time as possible.

"Table eighteen," Billy's dad told the hostess.

Smiling, the volunteer den mother led them over to a table where they picked up their salads and chose the dressing they wanted. Then, she directed them to their table, which had three empty spots.

Laughing and talking about the cute way the Scouts had come up with for seating them—"a table for three"—Leah didn't immediately notice the fourth person at their section of the banquet table.

It was Matt. She was so startled, she forgot her role of mother hen.

Ethan pulled out a chair for her, and luckily she remembered how to sit.

Annie sat two seats down from her,

Ethan in between them. Fortunately Leah hadn't needed to push them together.

"Hello," she greeted Matt, smoothing her skirt, conscious that she was more dressed up than usual.

"Evening."

She craned her head, searching. "Danny's excited, isn't he?"

"Yes."

"Is he serving this table?"

He glanced over at Ethan. "Nope."

Monosyllabic answers. "Are you okay?"

"Just came from work. Had a lot of correspondence to deal with."

She tilted her head toward Ethan and Annie slightly, then leaned close to Matt and lowered her voice. "They make a great couple, don't they?"

He stared at her in surprise. "I suppose."

She noted he was still on his salad, so he hadn't been there long, either. "So, what happens next?"

"One of the Scouts will come and ask what you want to drink and bring garlic cheese bread."

"I don't suppose there's a drink menu." She laughed, trying to break the tension she sensed in him.

"This isn't L.A. You remember L.A.? Land of big deals? Your family specializes in them, don't they?"

Her smile faded. For some reason his words hurt more than they should have. He hadn't snapped, but there had been an undercurrent, barely perceptible, in his tone. Glancing around, she looked for someone she recognized, someone else she could talk to besides him. She didn't know anyone else at their table other than Annie and Ethan, and she didn't want to interrupt them.

A young Scout approached. "Hi. Do you want something to drink?"

"That'd be great."

"Um. Water or punch?"

"Punch, please."

"Okay." He started to leave, then turned back. "Um. Do you want cheese bread?"

She smiled at the earnest youngster. "That sounds really good."

"Okay."

He left and she busied herself with the paper napkin in her lap.

Matt was still silent. Self-consciously, she ate her salad, scanning the crowd, wishing she could spot Danny. The room was noisy, especially since it seemed that most of Rosewood was packed inside. There was a lot of chatter, neighbors catching up with each other. Leah was glad to see that Ethan and Annie were caught up in conversation. She wouldn't interrupt even if no one spoke to her the rest of the evening. Which seemed highly possible with Matt seated next to her.

The Cub Scout returned with garlic cheese bread for her and Matt. An older Scout carried their punch.

"Ma'am, do you want your spaghetti with or without meat?" the older boy asked.

"What do you recommend?"

"I like the one with meat best."

"Then that's what I'll have." She smiled at the pair of boys.

"Mr. Whitaker?" the Scout asked.

"With meat, Randy."

Naturally Matt knew the boy's name.

Leah straightened in the folding chair and tried to look comfortable.

"The cheese bread's the best part." Matt's voice was quiet. Still, it startled her.

"Oh… Um, I haven't tried it yet." She opened the packet of aluminum foil and pulled a bit of the warm bread out and tasted it. "You're right. It's really good." She was so relieved he'd broken his silence. Even if the bread had tasted like cardboard, she'd have replied positively. Not that she appreciated the subtle sarcasm about her family's deal making. For just one evening she'd hoped there would be no tension between them. She'd thought things had improved since she'd told him Danny should stay in Rosewood, but maybe it was still too soon. She had no interest in fighting with Matt, though, so she kept to a neutral topic. "Looks like the Scouts will raise plenty of money for their equipment."

"They need a new trailer."

"Trailer?" She began picturing an open bed trailer, then a horse trailer…

"One to haul the camping equipment. The old one's too small and rusting out."

"I didn't know they needed a trailer, but then I've never been camping."

"It's for the long campouts when they carry a lot of supplies." He looked at her skeptically. "You've never been camping?"

She shook her head. "Nope. My dad's not really the camping type. We had all sorts of great weekends together but not camping. Does Danny enjoy it?"

"That's an understatement."

"I'd love to go on a campout with him."

"Hmm."

"What's that supposed to mean?"

"Nothing."

"You don't think I could handle it, do you?"

"People who haven't camped don't always have a realistic picture of what's involved."

"People?" Realizing she was raising her voice, she forced herself to speak more quietly. "You don't mean people, you mean me."

"You *are* a city person—"

Leah forgot about her resolve not to be

baited. "I'm getting tired of hearing that. When's your next available weekend?"

"Why?"

"I want to take Danny camping."

He raised his eyebrows.

"And you're invited," she continued.

"Big of you."

"I'm serious. I want to be more than a visitor in his life."

Matt glanced down the table.

Leah followed his gaze, reminded of her friends' presence, but they were absorbed in their own conversation. "Well?"

"And if you hate camping?"

"Then I'll stick it out."

"It could be miserable."

If he made it that way. So they were back to his favorite subject, what she was made of. "Like I said, I'll stick it out."

"Next weekend then."

Chapter Fourteen

Danny was so excited that Matt didn't have the heart to say anything negative about the trip. They'd taken other kids camping with them, but this was the first time they'd brought a lady along.

The cupcake lady as Danny still sometimes referred to her.

They left on Friday as soon as school was out. Matt had put the camper shell on his truck and it was already packed. He'd stopped earlier at the B and B for Leah's things. She'd bought her own tent and sleeping bag, along with a few other items he'd suggested on a list, but Matt had the rest of the equipment they'd need. They'd agreed that he would be in charge of the food supplies, even though she insisted on paying for half. She'd baked brownies and cookies, but otherwise he was surprised to see she'd packed light.

As they headed toward one of their favorite spots, Danny talked nonstop about the lake, fishing, hiking and telling campfire stories.

Unlike the mountains that ridged western Texas, the hill country rolled gently. Tucked away amid the clustered trees and open fields was the small lake they sought.

Once they arrived at their destination, Leah insisted on helping to unload the equipment. After securing Hunter, Matt and Danny went to work setting up camp. They always brought a large main tent that could be used for meals and recreation if the weather turned bad, plus a smaller tent to sleep in.

He glanced over at Leah, who was taking her brand-new tent out of its box. "You need help pitching your tent?"

"Um. No." She was reading the instruction booklet.

"Okay."

He and Danny pounded in stakes, securing the main tent.

"Maybe we should help her," Danny whispered.

"Give her a chance first," Matt replied quietly.

They pitched their second tent, put in the air mattresses and sleeping bags. Then they set up the camp tables and stove. Matt glanced at Leah occasionally as he unloaded the rest of the gear. She had the rear of the small tent erected, but it was sagging. Of course, it wasn't easy to pitch a tent while trying to read the directions.

Danny came to her rescue, showing her how to place the middle pole.

"The man at the hardware store said this tent was an easy one to put up," she said.

Danny shrugged. "Yeah, it is sorta. But it's not the kind that just pops open."

"Oh." She looked over at Matt and his tent. "Yours isn't, either, is it?"

"No. But we've done it bunches of times before." Danny helped her finish putting up the tent, then staked it.

"Thanks."

"S'okay. You'll do better next time."

She smiled ruefully. "I'll certainly try."

Danny put an air mattress in her tent.

"I didn't bring that."

"Dad packed it for you."

Matt dumped firewood next to a pit lined with the remains of old ashes, then dusted his hands. "The ground gets awfully hard."

Her expression lightened.

He didn't want to dwell on the difference her smile made to his mood as he squatted to build the fire.

"What can I do?" she asked.

"Hang out with Danny."

"Really?"

"We're set until supper, and it just has to cook once I get the fire going."

"Shouldn't I help prepare the food?"

"First night's easy. Dinner in foil packets in the campfire. And you already made dessert."

Her delight was as simple to read as a first-grade primer. "If you're sure..."

"Yes." Danny knew to stay within the parameters of the camp, not to wander too far. Still… "It'll start to get dark in about an hour, so—"

"Don't go too far." She pulled a compass from one pocket and pedometer from the other. "I came prepared to make sure we don't."

After he built the fire and put the foil packets of food at its base to cook, he settled back. Once the fire was established, he felt camp was set. The meat and vegetables in the packets would roast, giving them a hearty meal.

The skies were clear, and the weather forecast promised good weather. Should be nothing to worry about. But it seemed strange for Danny to be in someone else's care for the moment. Especially Leah's.

Well before the sun torched a path toward the horizon, they returned, their canvas bags filled with sticks for tomorrow's fire.

Relaxed, laughing, happy. It amazed Matt how natural they were together, as though the birth connection had somehow remained alive, strong.

"Something smells wonderful," Leah

declared, pulling off the backpack of wood. "And the fire looks great. I insist on doing all the cleanup tonight."

Danny began giggling all over again.

"What?"

"There isn't any cleanup the first night," Matt explained. "We just crumple up the foil and put it in the garbage. But I'll keep your offer in mind for breakfast."

Leah reached over and tickled Danny. "Smart guy."

He just laughed even harder.

Matt watched them together throughout dinner. As darkness settled over the land, their campsite seemed a more intimate space. Fallen logs made good seating around the fire as they toasted marshmallows and told scary stories.

As the appointed storyteller, he was amused to see that Leah's eyes were nearly as wide as Danny's when the story came to its climax. And when he reached out to spook Danny at the end, she jumped, as well, almost falling off the log. Then they both dissolved into laughter. Danny, not content to leave Matt out, tickled him, as well, and even Hunter joined in, barking at everyone.

"You're supposed to be scared," Matt gasped, moving out of reach.

"We were!" Leah scrambled to her feet. "But now we're paying you back," she teased.

"Truce!" He held up his hands. "I know where the hot cocoa is."

She looked at Danny. "Think we should let him off?"

"Yeah. I want cocoa."

Grinning to himself, Matt uncovered the packets that were in the food box. The tin coffeepot, filled with water, was already on the Coleman stove.

Leah located mugs and spoons and started snipping marshmallows into small pieces.

"I guess this doesn't exactly seem like roughing it." Looking sheepish, she held up a pair of tiny, folding scissors. "But I don't travel anywhere without these."

"Relax. The written test isn't until the *end* of the trip."

She grinned back at him.

Danny's eyelids started drooping before his cocoa was gone.

Matt draped an arm on his shoulders. "Hey, pal, how 'bout tucking in for the night?"

Danny struggled to stay awake, not wanting to miss anything. "It's not late."

"We've got the whole weekend ahead of us. You don't want to be too tired to enjoy it."

The little boy took one half-hearted sip of cocoa. "Okay."

Leah gently took his mug. "Good night, Danny."

"'Night."

Matt tucked him in, securing him in his sleeping bag. He smoothed back the hair on his forehead, knowing the boy was exhausted from the big day.

"Bless Daddy," Danny mumbled.

Matt knew he was almost asleep, that evening prayers wouldn't be complete tonight.

"An' bless Leah. Thanks for givin' Daddy somebody to love."

The fire snapped outside the tent, the

sound sharp in the silence Matt felt in his heart. *Was this what his son had been praying for?*

Hunter whined, butting his head at the sleeping bag so that he could lie next to Danny.

Matt stayed in the tent as long as he could—when he finally went back outside, Leah looked up at him. Her face, illuminated by the glow of the fire, was anxious.

"Is he okay?"

Matt nodded, then cleared his throat. "Just tired. Big day for him."

"Right. And me, I'm so wound up I'm sure I won't be able to go to sleep."

"Oh?"

"Afraid so." She hugged her knees. "To be able to spend so much time with Danny…" She glanced toward the tent, lowering her voice. "Is he asleep?"

Matt nodded.

"I can't explain how much this means to me…how much hope I have… I know this campout wasn't your idea, but I really appreciate being able to share this experience with Danny. I…" Woodsmoke floated between them. "Before…before I found Danny, I used to imagine how he'd turned out. I thought about sports and boy things and all that. I wondered what he liked, what he didn't like. But I never imagined…" She looked at him earnestly. "He's so…perfect."

Matt thought so, too. He also remembered the prayer he'd just heard. "No one's perfect."

She shook her head. "Maybe I'm not explaining it right. I feel like I did after I counted all his fingers and toes when he was born and saw that he was healthy. It wouldn't have mattered if he hadn't been beautiful, or if he'd been born with flaws or a handicap—to me he was perfect. And that's how he is now, how he's turned out…how he's been raised."

Speechless, he stared into the fire, then held out his hand.

She accepted it.

The words were hard for him to say, especially since he still had so many doubts about her. Ones he wasn't certain he could ever overcome. "This is a partnership that I never expected, that I'm still not sure about."

Her fingers curled within his hand. "Then let me prove to you it's one that will work."

Leah dreamed of the spa in Beverly Hills that gave the best facials in Southern California. Mudpacks, wraps, salt rubs that had their clientele begging just to be put on waiting lists. But she had reached the top of that list. Her facial was exquisite. Fingers were massaging her skin, moistening it, sanding it, licking it…

Licking it?

Giggles made her open one eye and squint into the light. What in the world?

Hunter, deciding she was free game, lapped at her face, lavishing her with doggie kisses.

"Are you awake?" Danny asked in a mock whisper that could have been heard at least two tents away.

"Oh, yeah." She struggled to sit up in her sleeping bag while the determined dog kept licking her face.

"Breakfast is ready."

"Oh, no!" She had planned to be up early, to make the meal, or at the least to help.

"Dad probably won't make you eat all of yours."

She grinned. What a wonderful way to wake up.

Matt stood at the stove piling eggs onto plates. "'Morning."

"'Morning. Sorry I'm a slug."

"It's okay. You're on KP anyway."

She headed toward the aroma of coffee, although the fresh air was more than enough of a wake-up. Grabbing a mug, she filled it and then joined the males at the table.

"What's on the agenda for today?"

"Hiking. Up for that?"

"I'm up for anything." She felt like she could climb mountains, swim oceans. But a hike was good. She'd checked out every book in the Rosewood library on camping and hiking, including both the Girl and Boy Scout Handbooks. She'd bought the right shoes for hiking. And socks. They'd also been on Matt's list. She'd been cramming for this trip from the moment Matt had agreed to it. She'd even selected the tent based on what she'd seen in the books. Apparently she should have gone with the one that just popped into place—the one the man in the hardware store had suggested—if she'd wanted to impress Matt. But something told her it would take far more than that to impress him.

Eager to begin their hike, Leah whizzed through the cleanup. With all the food, coolers and garbage secured in the truck's camper shell, they headed out.

Danny and Matt both had well-used walking sticks that Matt had carved. She was surprised when Matt handed her one, obviously new. She suspected that in his shop it would sell for a high price. One of the books she'd consulted had said to cut a stick in the woods. "Thank you. I didn't expect—"

"I know. But you'll find it makes the hike a lot easier."

The wood was smooth beneath her fingers as they walked, and it warmed under the persistent sun. Accustomed to an hour at the gym every day in L.A., she wasn't winded when they took their first break on an outcropping of rocks shaded by trees that grew farther up the hill.

Taking off her hat, Leah bathed her face with some of her drinking water. The curse of fair skin was that she flushed so quickly. But her energy was still high.

The wildflowers that covered the hillsides were breathtaking. Some delicate in color. Some, like the orange paintbrush, as bold as the state itself. They stayed on the trails where possible so they wouldn't crush the unspoiled blooms.

"Everything's so vast," Leah wondered aloud, seeing the miles of virgin land that stretched out before them. "That no one else has been on this path yet this spring, stepped among these flowers…it's amazing."

"The world is a big place," Matt replied.

And yet she'd found Danny.

The trail steepened and Matt held out a hand to help her climb. She didn't really need his help, yet she took it. And she didn't question why. Nor did she release his hand too quickly.

Or his gaze when it touched on hers longer than it had to. It wasn't thirst that dried her throat.

Nearly an hour later they came to a fork. Matt turned toward her. Then he frowned. "Where's your hat?"

Automatically, she reached toward the top of her head, but the hat was gone. All she felt was her hair pulled back into a ponytail. "I had it."

"Did you take it off?"

"I don't think so…I… Yes! I took it off when we had our break."

His frown deepened. "You're getting sunburned. We'd better turn back."

Danny let out a cry of distress.

"Danny," Matt cautioned.

"We don't have to go back!" Leah thought quickly. "I'll just keep putting on sunscreen."

"Do you have some with you? I didn't bring any because we're wearing hats and long-sleeved shirts."

"Sure. No reason to turn back." She

smiled brightly despite the fib, remembering plenty of hikes when she was younger. She hadn't had a hat or sunscreen and she'd been fine. And she wasn't going to spoil this outing for Danny.

Matt looked at her closely. "I guess so."

"Goody!" Danny was already turning back to the trail, Hunter bouncing along beside him on his leash.

The climb to the crest where they were eating lunch was strenuous but the view was worth it. White-tailed deer scattered as they entered a clearing, but they were close enough to see a wide-eyed doe and her fawn before they took flight.

Matt shrugged out of his backpack, the one containing most of the food. Leah's pack, like Danny's, was much lighter. Again she used her drinking water to bathe her face, hoping to cool down.

When she turned around, Matt was frowning again. "Are you sure your sunscreen's working? You look pretty red."

"I always flush from the heat. It's my Irish ancestry showing. Nothing to worry about."

But she could feel the sting in her cheeks and hoped that some of it might really be caused by exertion. That morning she'd been in such a rush to get going that she'd forgotten to put on any sunscreen at all. And there hadn't been any point in wearing makeup. But she wasn't going to wimp out and let Danny down.

During lunch she forgot about the heat, revitalized by granola bars, dried fruit and jerky.

"Not far now to the caves." Matt put on his backpack. "Just over the ridge."

She had mixed feelings about the caves. They would be cool and dark inside, but there might also be bats. Ugh.

Danny, on the other hand, was thrilled. "The caves are way cool, Leah."

"I'll bet," she said, trying to sound enthused.

The caves were worse than she'd expected, dark and narrow, with barely enough room for her and Matt to stand up straight. Leah was afraid she'd scrape her head against the ceiling, getting bats' wings or something equally unappealing in her hair.

Shuddering, she fell into line behind Matt as he and Danny led the way, side by side, into the cave, Hunter following quietly, subdued by this strange new place.

The beams from their flashlights bounced off walls so dark they were beyond black. The cavern gradually widened, the stone ceiling sloping upward, growing higher. Water dripped down on them. At least Leah hoped it was water. She couldn't see anything in the gloom.

She licked her lips, remembering she was thirsty. Momentarily distracted, she forgot about following Matt's exact steps. She couldn't have deviated much, but suddenly she felt something brush against her forehead, her face.

She screamed as bats flew past, their furry bodies and wings whipping around her head.

Matt turned and she lurched toward him. He stretched out his arms and she jumped into them, hanging on tight. A split second later she screamed for Danny and pulled him into their circle. While she hung on for dear life, she felt them shaking—not with fear, she finally realized, but laughter. Hunter barked furiously, running in circles, tangling his leash around their legs.

When the bats had passed them, Leah disentangled herself. She shone her flashlight from face to face. Matt was doing a better job of containing his amusement than Danny. One part of her wanted to hang on to her dignity, the other to blast them. But they'd almost been swarmed by bats. Gross, nasty bats.

Matt cleared his throat. "Are you okay?"

"What do you think?"

"Uh, I think you've never had that particular experience before."

She looked down at Danny.

"You can really jump *fast!*" he said with admiration.

She could stay mad, but instead she hooted with laughter. "I guess I can. But any more bats and I'm outta here."

Although they didn't have any further encounters, Leah was relieved when they finished exploring and made it back to the bright sunshine. They'd only been inside the cave a short time, but it was way too long for her.

"You'll get used to it," Danny told her. "First time's always hardest."

What a good boy he was. And he spoke with such assurance that there would be more of these outings with her.

"Time to head back," Matt announced.

"Aw, Dad."

Matt turned to Leah. "He'd say that if we hiked to San Antonio."

The sun was still high and hot as they headed down. The trail was a challenging one, but Leah didn't have any trouble, thanks to the sturdy hiking shoes and thick socks Matt had specified. She had wondered if he would try to sabotage her on this trip. It would have been easy enough to do. Instead, he'd made sure she had all the proper equipment, even offering to provide her tent and sleeping bag. It was the kindness in him, she realized, and the goodness. Even though he believed that she hadn't told the truth about Kyle, he wouldn't do anything to harm her.

She stumbled and Matt turned back,

holding his hand out. She took it, steadying herself.

"Tired?"

"No, just thinking."

"About?"

"Ironically, what great hiking shoes I'm wearing."

"They don't leap tall buildings or sticks in the trail, though."

"Nice way of saying I need to pay attention."

"You've done fine."

"Just *fine?*"

"No whining, no asking for special treatment. No real girly stuff."

She laughed. "Except for screaming and jumping into your arms in the cave. But I still contend bats go way beyond just girly." She shuddered. "Yuck, gross."

"No more caves for you?"

"I didn't say that."

"You've got pluck, Leah." He shook his head. "That's what my mother called it."

Touched, she swallowed. "That's the nicest thing you've ever said to me."

He drew his eyebrows together. There

was surprise in his eyes. And doubt. She wondered at its cause.

"Dad, Leah! Look, foxes!"

They both turned to see. Dainty, graceful and strong. And then the animals were gone.

And so was the moment.

The day was uncommonly hot, and her water was nearly gone. Bathing her face with it had used up her supply. By the last break she was so thirsty she sucked her lips in to hide their cracked appearance.

But Matt noticed. "Your sunscreen's no good." He pulled off his hat. "Wear this."

"No. I'm the one who lost my hat." And they hadn't found it on the way back. The wind or an animal must have knocked it from the trail.

He plopped it on her head. "No arguments. You're red as a late summer tomato."

Since even her eyeballs felt hot and her head was beginning to throb, she complied. At least the trail was getting easier, flattening out more.

The last hour Leah's face and neck seemed to be on fire. Her energy was sapping, but she concentrated on Danny's happy voice. She had to admit that the camp looked decidedly wonderful when they reached it, though.

Shrugging off her backpack, she collapsed on the log near the blackened fire pit. If not for Danny, she would have crawled into her tent and closed her eyes until morning.

Miraculously, he and Matt were puttering around camp, starting a new fire, preparing for dinner, acting as though they hadn't hiked a zillion miles. She knew she should stir, but her legs felt like rubber.

Matt tapped on her hat. Well, his hat.

"You under there?"

She nodded.

He added wood to the pit to rekindle the fire he'd carefully banked that morning. "You're awfully quiet."

She nodded again.

"Something wrong?"

Leah started to shake her head, but the motion sent the throbbing behind her eyes into full gear and she reached up to grab the sides of her head, encumbered by the hat.

"Leah?" Concerned, he tipped the hat back from her forehead. "Leah!"

She knew her face must look half-cooked by the day in the sun. Her lips, swollen and cracked, were difficult to move. "What?"

"You're burned to bits. What kind of sunscreen were you using?"

She closed her eyes, the movement painful. "I didn't actually have any."

"What?"

"I was afraid you'd make us turn back if you knew I didn't have any sunscreen after I went and left my hat on a rock."

"But…why?"

"I didn't want to disappoint Danny."

"He'd have gotten over it," Matt said in exasperation.

Her vision was swimming. She wasn't certain if it was tears or light-headedness. Her throat felt so dry. "But this was so special to me."

"You beat all." He laid the back of his hand on her forehead.

A tear slipped from her eyes. "I read all the books."

"What books?"

"From the library. On camping and hiking. And the Scout manuals. I wanted to do everything right."

He smoothed the tears from her cheeks, his touch gentle. "It's not worth crying over."

"I didn't think I'd lose my hat."

"Can't really tell if you have a fever," he muttered. "Your whole face is burned. So's your neck." He picked up her pack and shook her water bottle. "Empty. You probably used more of it cooling down your face than drinking it. I don't know what to make of you. All so Danny wouldn't be disappointed. What if you'd had a heat stroke? That can be fatal, you know."

"But Danny—"

"Would be disappointed, I know." He dipped his bandanna in cool water and laid it on her forehead. "I imagine he'd be pretty disappointed if you dropped dead out here, too."

She groaned.

He sighed. "That's not going to happen. You need to fill up on fluids." He reached for her arm. "Come on. Rest for you tonight."

"No," she pleaded. "I want to stay up with Danny."

"But—"

"Please. I don't want him to know I messed up again."

He wavered. Retrieving the water jug, he poured her a full cup. "Sip slow, but steady."

Another tear escaped, trickling down her burned cheek. "I feel so stupid."

He relented. "You're just a little too enthusiastic, sometimes."

Matt left her with the water. The first-aid kit contained burn medication, but he searched for a native plant that would work better. Finding an aloe vera, he cut off a stalk, slit off the thorny edges, then peeled back the outer layer to reveal the gooey pulp.

"Okay, Leah, this will feel kind of slimy but cool." She braced as though the cure would be worse than the burn. He was careful as he applied the transparent gel to her forehead. Her eyes were nearly level with his and she watched as his fingers moved over her cheeks, then eased down to her cracked lips. "There, that ought to do it." He kept his hand on her face a moment, reluctant to break the contact. Her eyes kept searching his. In them he saw questions and a vulnerability at odds with the strength she was always bent on proving. "I'd better get that fire started."

She was so close he could see her swallow. "Right." Her voice was husky. "Thanks."

"I'll cut some more aloe vera so you'll have plenty for tonight." He fumbled with the piece in his hand. "Now I'll get to that fire."

Danny and Hunter loped toward them, both arriving breathless. "You're awful red!"

"Too much sun today," she admitted.

"Your hat," he remembered.

"Yes. I shouldn't have left it on the trail. Pretty dumb, huh?"

"It's okay."

"You're very forgiving."

"Jesus forgives us so we're supposed to forgive others." He shrugged. "Even yourself."

She reached out and hugged him, sunburn and all.

Matt turned away, the clutch of emotion as powerful as a home run hit miles out of the park.

By morning Leah felt better. Matt's care was responsible. He'd kept applying the pulp of the aloe vera plant on her face and neck, all the while insisting that she keep drinking water. As she rehydrated, her headache faded and her body began to feel normal again. He was even sensitive to the fact that the campfire would hurt her sunburn, so they sat around the table instead.

And he'd insisted on cooking breakfast without her help, cleaning up the same way. So she sat now at the table, watching as he and Danny put away the cooking gear.

"Leah, we have our own kind of service on Sundays when we camp, nothing formal, just our own thing. Do you feel up to walking down to the lake?"

She waved her hands. "I'm no wilting buttercup. And the lake's within sight. Besides, I feel much better this morning."

"Okay." He picked up his Bible, handing her his hat to wear. Together, along with Hunter, they strolled to the shore of the small lake. The morning was cool and trees shaded the grassy area they stood on.

Matt opened with a prayer, then Danny sang in a sweet clear voice the well-known verses of "Jesus Loves Me."

Matt hesitated a moment. "Would you like to read the Bible passage for us, Leah?"

She trembled from nerves, then nodded. "Yes." She accepted the outstretched Bible and turned to the one passage that she remembered well, that she had read often when Danny was missing.

"This is from Luke 18— '*And they brought unto him also infants, that he would touch them; but when his disciples saw it, they rebuked them. But Jesus called them unto him, and said, Suffer little children to come unto me, and forbid them not: for of such is the kingdom of God.*'"

When she finished, she looked at Matt

to see if she had done all right. Was that approval in his gaze?

"Now we tell what we've had to be thankful for," Matt explained. "Danny, do you want to begin?"

He nodded. "I'm thankful for Hunter....

Leah and Matt smiled.

"And my dad and Leah...."

She swallowed.

"And all my friends, especially Billy and his new brother or sister."

Matt looked at Leah.

"I have so many things to be grateful for," she said, struggling to steady her voice. "My parents, their love and support. Good friends. The special people who've come into my life here in Rosewood." She drew another calming breath. "Danny and his father, my friend Annie." She didn't meet Matt's gaze.

The gentle breeze stirred the leaves.

"I'm thankful for my son," Matt began. "For all he brings to my life, for the joy he gives me. And I'm thankful to the Lord for His blessings. They're constant, never failing."

Surrounded by the beauty of the countryside, Leah considered the source of Matt's unwavering faith. Faith so great it baffled and humbled her.

Chapter Fifteen

"Sounds like the trip was a huge success." Annie refilled their orange juice glasses. Her other guests had already left for the day, wanting an early start on the nearby wildflower trails that filled the hill country and drew visitors to Rosewood.

Leah felt the warmth that had stayed with her since Matt and Danny had dropped her off the previous evening. "It was good. Really good. How about you? Did you see Ethan?"

"At church. Oh, Leah, I like him so much. I just never hoped…"

The nudging was paying off.

"I almost forgot. Your mother called twice."

Leah frowned. Her mother was becoming more and more insistent. "What did you tell her?"

"That you were out looking at wildflowers. I felt funny not coming clean. I mean, it wasn't *exactly* a lie. I knew you were bound to be looking at wildflowers at some point on the campout, but…"

"It wasn't squeaky clean, either. I'm sorry. I didn't mean to stick you in the middle, but I'm not ready to tell my parents what I've decided."

"What *have* you decided?"

Leah gazed out the large window that overlooked the peaceful backyard. Songbirds perched on the sturdy limbs of the old magnolia tree, hopping over to the well-stocked feeder. "Annie, have you ever thought of leaving here? Starting over somewhere completely new?"

"Sure. I thought maybe if I left, I could put this—whatever it is that makes such bad things happen in my family—behind me. But this is all I know. Rosewood is where my friends are. It takes courage to start somewhere new, more than I've got. Even though I understand why you had to come here, I don't think I could do what you have. Jumping right in at the school, volunteering…not knowing anybody."

"It's not courage, Annie, it's…Danny's mine, even though I'm the worst mother on the planet—"

"That's not true!"

Touched by her friend's loyalty, Leah patted Annie's hand. "It's not just what I've done, it's what I haven't done."

Perplexed, Annie waited.

"I haven't figured out how to tell Danny who I am."

"Well, it'll take time."

"But will the news get any easier to take?" she wondered aloud. "I mean…it's going to be a shock no matter when he hears it. Will it be worse now or when he knows me better?"

"When he *likes* you better, you mean."

Leah ducked her head. "Is that wrong?"

"I don't know. He's *your* child. What do you think?"

"He likes me now." She felt the warmth of his hug, the joy of his laughter, the promise in his eyes. "That I'm fairly certain of. And I think his feelings for me are growing. But I also think it's too early to test them."

Annie fiddled with the handle on the juice pitcher. "So, what are you going to tell your parents when they call again?"

"I told them I'd be home well before my birthday."

"Is that soon?"

"Next week." Leah sighed. "Which isn't any big deal, except that I made it into one. I told them I was determined to have Danny home with me by then."

"Still planning to be in L.A. for the festivities?"

"No. I'll find a way to explain to my parents."

"So what day next week?"

"Saturday. Why?"

"Just wondering."

"Don't make a fuss, Annie."

"I think we have all the fuss going on we need already, thank you."

"Good. Because this is the birthday nobody believes—my twenty-ninth. Everybody's always twenty-nine! I'd sooner skip the groans of disbelief."

"That you're twenty-nine not twenty-one."

Annie's smile was so genuine that Leah rolled her eyes. "Fine, cake. You and me. But that's it!"

Leah managed to avoid her mother's phone calls for more than a week, but she was squeezing Annie into a corner. And her friend was running out of excuses for why Leah wasn't returning messages from the inn or on her cell phone.

And with her birthday only days away, her time of grace was just about up. So when her cell phone rang as she walked down Main Street, she gritted her teeth and answered the call.

"At last! I thought you'd gone underground! If that's possible in the middle of nowhere."

"Only if you're a prairie dog, Mother."

"Is that some sort of Texas humor?"

"I suppose. So, how are you?"

"Getting frantic to be truthful. Not being able to contact my only child for more than a week..."

Oh, this was high drama. "Now, Mother, you know I left messages on your voice mail."

"When you knew I wouldn't be there! It's as though you deliberately didn't want to talk to me." The pouting came through, loud and clear.

"Mother, I have decisions to make—"

"So what are you planning to do? Hang around in that little town until you reach an agreement with this man?"

She hedged. "Something like that."

"Leah, how can you possibly expect that to work? The boy needs to know how his life is going to be structured so he can adjust. If you're confused, he'll feel it."

She took a deep breath. "Mother, I'm working things out, but nothing's settled yet. And it won't be for a while."

"How long a while?" Rhonda's voice gathered suspicion.

"I don't really know. But don't make

any plans with me in them, starting with my birthday."

"Starting?"

"Like I said, it's going to take a while."

"I don't like the sound of this, Leah."

"You'll probably want to shift my client base to Edward."

"Leah!"

"For now, Mother. Some of the accounts need more personal attention than Jennifer can give them. Until I make a permanent decision, I think that's best."

"It sounds like you've already made one, and it doesn't bode well."

"No, I'm trying to make one. It's...difficult."

"To bring home your child? How can that be?"

"It's complicated, Mother."

"You have the best lawyers at your disposal. Use them."

How could she explain it wasn't a legal issue? "Mother—"

"You said you could fight this on your own. But your father and I can be on the next plane out—"

"No!"

"Really, Leah, this is the time for family to stick together."

"I can handle it, Mother. I don't need a show of Hunter power."

"Why not bring the boy's uncle back to L.A., too?"

Leah sighed. That would be like uprooting a hickory tree and expecting it to flourish on one of L.A.'s freeways. "I don't think so."

"Are you trying to make it impossible to come home?"

"Of course not. I'm just trying to explain why it's difficult, complicated, why it's going to take longer than I thought."

"We could help make it easier, Leah."

She clutched the phone closer. "I know you want to help. But let me do this."

"Your birthday, sweetheart. All alone in a strange town…"

"Hardly. I've made friends. Annie, who runs the B and B, is making a cake from an old family recipe, my favorite. She's great. You'd like her."

"You have friends here," Rhonda reminded her.

"I have room in my life for both."

"I thought this trip was about Danny."

"It is. Annie's an unexpected blessing."

"Blessing?" Surprise coated the word. But then it hadn't been in Leah's vocabulary before.

"I've discovered quite a few in Rosewood."

"I see."

Leah wondered what exactly her mother was picturing at the moment—what her daughter had gotten involved in. "It'll be okay, Mother. Trust me."

Rhonda sighed. "It sounds like I'll have to."

It wasn't a vote of confidence, but it would do.

Leah didn't mind helping Emma with inventory at the costume shop. In fact, usually it was a lot of fun, but trying on half a dozen costumes wasn't her favorite thing. And this last one...Cinderella. Leah felt like she ought to be climbing into a pumpkin any minute. Emma had insisted she put on the whole getup, and then she'd rushed over to the B and B to meet with her client, the one who was going to sponsor the costumes for the school's next play. She planned to bring him over to the shop for a preview.

The phone rang and Tina answered. "Are you sure? Well, why can't you come over here? You want me to wear *what?* I guess so. But you owe me big."

"What's wrong?"

Tina clicked off, looking disgusted. "Our sponsor has a sprained ankle and wants us to trot over to the B and B wearing our costumes."

"Our?"

Tina grimaced. "She expects me to put on that blasted Tinker Bell outfit."

Leah barely covered her laugh with a cough that came out sounding more like a croak.

"Go ahead and laugh," Tina muttered, grabbing the offending costume and heading into the dressing room. She continued grumbling but was out in a remarkably short time. "Might as well get this over with. Ready, Cinders?"

"Ready, Tinker."

Feeling a little ridiculous in a ballgown, not to mention tiara, wand and silver shoes, Leah walked the short distance down Main Street with Tina. This same sponsor apparently donated a small fortune to the local theater so it was well worth the temporary discomfort for the school coffers. But the two of them collected a few odd looks.

"We should have taken the pumpkin," Leah muttered. "Less conspicuous."

"I hate to hitch up the mice for these short jaunts," Tina replied.

"True." Leah pushed in the latch to open the front door of Borbey House.

"Surprise!"

Truly, completely surprised, Leah stood stock still, her mouth ajar. Streamers, balloons and crepe paper decorated the entryway.

"Happy birthday!" The wishes came at her from all sides as people dressed in costumes popped out of their hiding places, then drew her into the room.

Tina, Emma and Annie wore matching conspiratorial grins.

But then, Leah couldn't stop smiling, either. "I can't believe you pulled this off—that I fell for your plan."

"It was easy," Annie admitted. "I think it was decorating the cake in front of you, and renting the movie you wanted. You figured I was planning a simple celebration for the two of us."

"It's that innocent look of yours," Leah teased.

Tina grinned at her. "I couldn't believe it when Emma got you to put on the Cinderella gown."

"And on my birthday." Leah groaned. "I must have seemed like the perfect dupe."

Tina held up her camera. "Let's just say we're glad we have pictures."

It seemed as if everyone Leah had met from the church and school was crowded into the B and B. She couldn't believe they'd all turned out for her birthday. Emma and her family. Ethan and the rest of the artistic committee. Principal Gunderland, Miss Randolph, several other teachers, Cindy Mallory, even the pastor, Katherine Carlson, and her family. Leah's eyes scanned the group. There they were, Danny and Matt. Leave it to Annie!

"Hey, Leah!" Danny hollered.

"Hey, Danny!" She grinned and waved.

He waved back, heading toward her.

Matt wasn't far behind. He looked so handsome. Dressed as Indiana Jones, Danny as the child who'd aided the action hero on his quest. Actually feeling like Cinderella, Leah caught her breath. "Don't you look…wonderful!"

"So do you!" Danny's eyes shone.

She bent to kiss his cheek.

"Yes," Matt said quietly.

Rising, she met his gaze. "Thank you."

"Happy birthday!" Danny chirped.

"Thank you again. I can't believe this party."

"You're really surprised?" Matt asked.

"Absolutely. I *saw* Annie making the cake from her special recipe. And she rented my favorite movie. This…this… Well, she really got me."

"We knew all along," Danny confided.

"Then you're really good at keeping secrets. I'm terrible at it." She glanced at Matt, wondering at the strange expression that flashed in his eyes.

"What we got you for your birthday is a secret, too," Danny told her.

Matt nudged him.

Leah smiled. "Oh, my."

"But I can't tell you what it is," Danny continued.

"Of course not." She smoothed the diaphanous folds of her gown, then glanced at Matt. "You didn't have to get me a present."

"Sure we did," Danny declared. "You always bring a present to a birthday party."

His simple truths were constantly amazing her.

"Just like you always get cake," he explained.

"Sounds like a fair exchange to me," she observed.

Danny glanced toward the other kids Annie had included in the party.

"If it's all right with your dad, you can go and play with your friends, Danny."

"Okay," Matt agreed, and the boy took off.

Despite the noise that filled the room, an awkward silence fell between them.

"Well," Matt said at last.

"Yes?"

"Are you missing your family?"

Surprisingly she wasn't. "No. As I was telling Annie, this is the birthday no one believes, my twenty-ninth. People always think you're holding out on the thirtieth."

"I'd forgotten you told me when you met John you were only—"

"Nineteen, just barely. With all the sense of a peanut." She laughed softly. "That seems like a hundred years ago."

"Do you wish you'd never met him?"

"If I hadn't, there'd be no Danny. I'd think you, of all people, would believe in greater plans."

"I do. But I got the best part of this plan."

She reached up to adjust her tiara. "Maybe I'm beginning to, as well."

Leaning forward, he closed his hand over hers, helping her right the crooked tiara. There was but a whisper between them, their gazes lingering.

Then he pulled back. "Your sunburn's all healed."

She lifted her hand to her face, remembering his tender touch, how he'd doctored her all through that night. She had counted only on herself since the day Danny had disappeared. She'd refused to trust, to lean on anyone. She'd never expected it to feel so good.

Several voices called her name.

"Your friends await, Cinderella," he said quietly.

"Right." Her ballgown rustled as she turned.

The house was filled with people, conversation and good food. The party seemed to go on and on. Danny stood at her side as she blew out her candles and cut the cake.

Then it was time for presents. Leah was overwhelmed. She was a newcomer to Rosewood, yet these people had taken her into their hearts, given her a place in their community, welcomed her as a friend.

"You really shouldn't have done this," she kept repeating as she unwrapped each gift.

A lace shawl from Emma. A vibrant silk purse Tina had made herself. A bracelet from Annie with a single charm engraved with one word: sisters. Leah found herself hugging everyone after each gift.

Danny was bouncing up and down when it came time for his and Matt's gift. Leah's hands were trembling as she opened the box. Nestled carefully inside was a perfectly carved heart locket on a slender gold chain, her initials across the front. She'd never before seen a locket carved of wood, but this one… Like any piece of fine jewelry, it opened seamlessly, and inside was a picture of Danny.

She smoothed her hands over the fine grained cherry wood. "It's beautiful…just beautiful. Thank you."

"Me and Dad made it. Well, mostly Dad."

"You both did a wonderful job." Her gaze moved up to include Matt, her heart catching. "Just wonderful."

"Danny wanted you to have something special."

She swallowed. "It's more special than I can say." Ignoring Matt's exclusion in the sentiment, she hugged her son. "The best present I've ever gotten."

Chapter Sixteen

Matt didn't even open the envelope. It was the third letter from Barrington Industries in only three weeks. There had been calls, too, requesting a meeting. He hadn't returned any. And Nan had said a man in an expensive looking suit had been asking for him in the store. He'd left a card. One of Barrington's representatives.

Matt didn't have to ask why they were so determined. Nor did he delude himself that he was a modern day Michelangelo and Barrington wanted exclusive rights.

The Hunters wanted Leah in L.A. And Danny, of course. Getting him there, too, would assure them that he wouldn't try to take his son back to the wilds of Texas, he supposed.

They liked being in control. That was what John had told him. They wanted to run things. John was supposed to work for them, live where he was told, do what he was told. He hadn't wanted to live his life that way and neither did Matt. He was surprised Leah did. And disappointed.

Yet despite knowing this, he was still drawn to her. His defenses were crumbling.

He tapped the envelope. Was this why John had run? Had he felt trapped by the Hunters? He'd been young. Had he thought there was no other way out?

Nan breezed in to the back room. "That man's on the phone again. Same one who's been calling all week."

He shook his head. "Not interested."

"Shouldn't you tell him that?"

"Just take a message, Nan."

"Okay."

He remembered Leah's determination on the hike, her concern that Danny not be disappointed. It seemed at odds with this plotting and planning. She'd still said nothing about the proposed buyout. Had she thought distancing herself from it would remove the taint of deceit?

It was the deceit that made him question her relationship with Danny and the wisdom of revealing who she was. He knew how badly she wanted Danny to know. He'd been praying about it, but the answer kept eluding him.

He didn't want to disappoint Danny. Learning Leah was his mother, then having her let him down…that would devastate his son.

It wasn't her occasional irresponsible behavior that led him to think that would happen, but this…this buyout offer. This deceit. Danny had so much trust, so much love to give.

Much like himself. He'd nearly let his resolve slip at Leah's birthday party. She'd made him want to forget old hurts, past differences as they'd laughed together at the Borbey House. She'd convinced him he'd held a genuine princess in his arms. But she was a princess with a secret agenda.

His sigh echoed in the empty room.

* * *

Leah's cell phone rang insistently as she walked to Borbey House. She took it from her purse, guessing who it was before she saw the readout. "Hello, Mother."

"Hello, dear. I've been calling and calling."

"I've been busy at the school. I had my phone turned off."

"There's not much point in carrying a cell phone if you're not going to answer it."

Leah counted to three. "Is something up?"

"Yes, darling. Westien Hotels just called."

"Oh."

"Is that all you can say? Leah, you worked for months to hook them. It's a huge entrée into the Scandinavian hotel business."

"I know. It just doesn't seem relevant right now."

"Not relevant? What's wrong with you?"

"I'm sorry, Mother, but I'm not thinking about clients these days."

"Is Danny all right?"

"He's fine."

"When will you two be coming home?"

Leah hedged. "Rosewood has been home to Danny all his life."

"But you can't just petrify out there, dear. Have you told Danny who you are yet?"

Leah fumbled with the phone, making a few buttons squawk.

"Leah?"

"No, Mother. I haven't told him yet."

"What are you waiting for?"

"The right moment."

"You need to bring him home."

It all seemed so black and white to her mother. Leah had tried talking to her father, who was more patient, but he was sticking with her mother on this one. He thought Leah should return to L.A. with Danny. As he put it: the boy had been gone long enough.

Leah did something she rarely liked to do. "You're breaking up, Mother. I'll talk to you later." She pushed the Off button, then snapped the phone shut. If someone needed her, they could call her at the B and B. She hardly used her cell phone in Rosewood, and it was an amazingly liberating experience.

Besides, she'd already planned to meet Danny and Matt at the drugstore for ice cream that evening. She grinned to herself, thinking of the high-maintenance places she'd gone to on dates in the city. Funny. None could compare to an evening on Main Street in Rosewood.

"Sprinkles?" Clyde, the clerk at the soda fountain, asked.

"Yes, please," Leah replied, as he built her banana split.

Danny dug into his double caramel and hot fudge sundae, which was loaded with cherries. "I got more cherries this time than ever!"

The clerk finished her sundae with a flourish of whipped cream and placed it on the marble counter in front of her.

"Ah. The touch of a master chef."

Hooking his feet over the stool, Danny leaned toward her. "The ice cream's already cooked."

She laughed, then hugged him. Not understanding the joke, he shrugged and turned back to his ice cream.

"You folks enjoy," the clerk said as he delivered Matt's sundae.

"Thanks, Clyde."

Leah glanced at his dish, then her own. "I feel kind of piggish. You didn't order nearly as much."

"I ate a steak for dinner. What did you have?"

She tried to remember. She'd been upset by her mother's phone call, then had to rush to meet them here. "Uh, seems I'm having it."

"Why don't you get a burger?"

"Then I wouldn't have room for all my ice cream. Besides, I have fruit, dairy, all the food groups I want right here."

"Want me to see if Clyde has some broccoli he can chop and sprinkle on top?"

"Gee, could you?"

Danny rolled his eyes. "You guys are silly."

Matt lifted the untouched cherry from his sundae and placed it on hers. "I seem to remember you like these better."

The simple gesture made her feel remarkably warm inside. "Yeah." She cleared the lump in her throat. "I do." She glanced over at Danny. "But I'm not the only one who likes them."

Danny shrugged. "It's okay. I got bunches." He took another bite of ice cream. "Are you goin' with us Saturday?"

"What's happening Saturday?"

"We're gonna go to the beach."

She glanced at Matt. "The beach? Aren't we quite a way from the ocean?"

"Galveston. It's about three and a half hours from here."

Was there hesitation in his voice? "Oh."

"I have to check out some special hardware a guy there produces by hand. Thought I might as well make a day of it with Danny. Would you like to come along? I have to warn you—we'll be leaving before dawn."

Which should she believe was genuine? The hesitation, the invitation or the warning?

"Yes, come!" Danny ignored his beloved cherries. "Please."

Her feelings pulled in opposite directions, she decided not to look at Matt again. "How can I say no?"

They reached the island city by daylight. Towering, fan-fringed palm trees and oleander bushes, ripe with fuchsia blooms, lined the center of Broadway. The wide boulevard ran through the center of the Victorian town, which was lined with mansions from its proudest era. Humid air carried the unmistakable tang of the ocean, of salt water, sand and tossing waves.

Inside the truck cab, the trio felt it. "Are we far from the beach, Dad?"

"Not too far. But we should have some breakfast, then swing by the hardware place. Get the business done first."

"Didn't you say the hardware place is on the Strand?" Leah shifted so she faced Matt.

"Yeah."

"Maybe there's a place close by where we can eat." She glanced down at Danny. "I did a little checking on the Internet. The Strand's supposed to be fun."

"Fine with me." He grinned at his son. "*And* it's in the same direction as the beach."

"Yay!"

The historic Strand district was once the heart of Galveston in the late 1800s and early 1900s. High curbs and overhanging canopies, meant to shade the streets, retained the charm of the era.

Leah was immediately captivated. "I love this!"

"They hold a Mardi Gras here every year, and at Christmas, Dickens on the Strand."

"I can see it now. With these Greek Revival and Victorian buildings…it must be fantastic."

"There was talk years ago of tearing this all down. But the historic society fought it, said it could be revived."

Leah shook her head. "Amazing. This area covers blocks, doesn't it? Now it's filled with stores and art galleries and restaurants. Good thing the historical society won. How do you know so much about it?"

"I've always liked Galveston. If it hadn't

been for the hurricane of 1900, it would have been the biggest city in the state instead of Houston. It's chock full of history. Not too far from here you can see what's left of the pirate Jean Lafitte's house." He motioned around them. "There's living history, beaches and seafood fresh off the boats."

She laughed. "What's *not* to like?"

"There's a real submarine in the park by the ferry," Danny told her. "And a battle-ship."

She turned in a semicircle, gazing at the fascinating pairing of old and new. "I could spend all day right here exploring shops and galleries."

Danny's expression filled with genuine alarm.

"Don't worry," she was quick to reassure him, not hiding her wide grin. "I won't."

They chose a breakfast spot that was housed in what had originally been a coffee importing warehouse. Now they sold small burlap sacks of coffee beans. More importantly, they served tasty and quick breakfasts.

When they were finished, they headed over to the hardware store. Hand-tooled knobs and drawer pulls fascinated the designer in Leah as Matt spoke to the owner about creating some pieces for an armoire he was designing. Danny fidgeted even though it didn't take long, his mind on beaches and submarines.

Luckily they weren't far from the seawall. The sound of the surf and seagulls could be heard despite the traffic as they drove alongside the ocean. Matt kept his speed down so they could breathe in the tangy sea air and admire the piers that jutted into the ocean. Some were used for fishing, others had restaurants or were crammed with chintzy souvenir shops. The ones that thrust farther out held elegant hotels.

Matt continued driving until they reached the turnoff to Stewart Beach. Leah didn't argue when Matt insisted on renting a beach umbrella because of her fair skin. She'd stuffed enough sunscreen into her beach bag for several people, but why take chances?

Matt took Danny to the bath house to change into their swim trunks. When they emerged, he was surprised to see Leah wearing her T-shirt and shorts. She walked out from beneath the umbrella to meet them. "Aren't you swimming?"

"I'm not a swimmer," she confessed. "I dip my toes in along the shore, but that's it."

"But you live by the ocean," Danny pointed out. "You shouldn't be scared of it."

"I'm not scared of the ocean."

"Danny, why don't you grab the bottle of sunscreen out of our beach bag," Matt suggested.

"Okay," he said, racing over to the umbrella, where Matt had left the bag.

"Diplomatic." Leah brushed sand from her shorts.

"Afraid of the water?"

"Always have been. My parents gave me lessons, but I wouldn't put my head under the water. So one of the teachers decided the baptism by fire method was the way to go. I nearly drowned. And now I have a deathly fear of deep water. My parents insisted I keep going to the lessons, even though I just kept sinking like a stone. I went through all the motions, but I've never been able to go in deep water since then. It terrifies me."

"So we'll stay by the shore."

"No! You and Danny go and swim. I'm fine. I won't drown dipping my toes in the shallow part. And I like to dig my feet into the sand. I can amuse myself doing that. If I get bored, I'll lie down in one of those chairs you rented and listen to the ocean. It's been awhile since I've heard the sounds of waves, you know."

"Yeah. Okay. Later, I'd thought about riding the ferry, but if that's going to bother you—"

"Not unless we have to swim for it."

He grinned. "I'm pretty sure that won't happen."

"Really, I love what I've seen of Galveston. It's just the deep water thing. Anything else is great."

Danny raced toward them with a bottle of sunscreen and handed it to her. "Will you do my back?"

"Sure."

When she'd finished, Danny turned and hugged her. "It's okay to be scared of the water," he whispered. "Everybody's scared of something."

Oh, how she loved this child. Then he was running toward the waves, Matt close behind.

She didn't want to transmit her fear to Danny, but she kept her eyes trained on him as they played in the surf. Matt was never more than a foot away, easily able to reach him if he needed to.

It seemed impossible to believe that they hadn't always been in her life, as important as both of them had become. She could see so much of Matt in Danny, but every now and then there was a glimpse of Kyle, as well. She supposed his memory would never completely disappear from their lives. And she wondered if it should. Children needed the truth. But she knew how the truth would hurt.

Retreating to the chairs beneath the umbrella, Leah continued to watch. She couldn't relax. Not while they remained in the water. Still, it was a beautiful day, the sun high in the cloudless sky.

There were plenty of people on the beach. Tourists had descended on Galveston like the sunshine and warm weather. Teenage girls walked by in pairs, giggling at teenage boys. And the surf was mild; swimmers carried inflatable toys, floats and beach balls.

Still, Leah felt huge relief when Danny and Matt headed for shore. She reached for the towels.

Laughing, Danny sprinkled her with water when he got close enough. She covered him with a towel. "Okay, smart guy." But she didn't mind.

"You want to build a sandcastle, Leah?" Danny asked, his voice muffled by the towel.

"Absolutely." She dried him off, then picked up the plastic bucket and shovel.

Matt dug in the cooler. "You two start. I'll get the drinks."

Danny grabbed her hand and they walked out to the damp sand and knelt down.

"This okay?" she asked, scooping up a bucketful of sand and upending it.

He patted the sand in place. "Yep. We'll need a big base."

They worked in silence for a few minutes. Matt brought sodas and joined the effort. While Leah formed turrets and a tower, she noticed that Danny was building a house that resembled his own.

Matt's large hands shaped the roof, occasionally grazing hers.

Leah tried not to make more of his touch than it warranted, but she found her gaze straying to his before she forced it back to the sandcastle.

"Hey, Leah, you just filled in the window."

"Sorry, sweetie." She dug the sand back out.

"When we finish this, you wanna look for shells?"

"I'm game."

"Dad?"

"Sure."

"I wish we could have brought Hunter along."

"He's fine at Roger's," Matt replied.

"He's romping with the other dogs, having a good old time. You wouldn't have been able to do everything you wanted to if we'd brought him."

"Yeah, I guess."

Danny was content with building the sandcastle, a search for shells, then another swim in the ocean. After oyster po'boys, they headed over to SeaWolf Park to tour the submarine.

The ferry was close by, so when they'd finished at the park, they drove over to the dock and parked. They walked onto the double-decker boat that made the crossing to Bolivar Island. Once the commuter ferry was filled with cars and passengers, it pulled away from the pier, a flock of seagulls following in its wake.

Many of the passengers congregated at the rear of the boat, tossing pieces of bread to the birds. The three of them had crusts from their lunch and Danny threw the bits skyward, delighted when a seagull swooped to catch the piece midair.

After a while, they walked to the prow of the ferry. Matt pointed to one of the huge ships in the distance. "Ocean liners. That one's Greek."

"I can't see," Danny complained.

Leah lifted him in front of her.

"Oh, yeah."

Grinning impishly, she held Danny's arms up in the pose that the movie *Titanic* had made famous, then motioned for Matt to get behind her, and all three of them assumed the stance.

Wind whipped through their hair and clothes. It was unexpected. It was silly. It was a memory moment.

The ship lurched slightly and Matt leaned in farther to steady her. Everything in that instant was perfect.

Chapter Seventeen

Billy's family was overwhelmed by the cradle. His father, Cal Mickleson, kept running his hands over the smooth wood.

His mother, Belinda, had tears in her eyes. "It'll become a family heirloom. It's so lovely."

"So much work you put into this," Cal murmured. "I don't have the words…."

Matt put his arm on his son's shoulder. "It was Danny's idea and we worked on it together."

"You've always been a wonderful friend to Billy, and now you'll be like another older brother to the baby." Belinda hugged Danny. "You've raised a wonderful boy," she said to Matt, including Leah in her smile.

"Yeah!" Billy jumped up. "We can share him!"

"Him?" Leah asked.

Belinda patted her stomach. "We just found out. Billy's going to have a little brother."

"Wow!" Danny's eyes were wide.

"That's wonderful," Leah murmured.

"Yes, great news," Matt agreed.

Leah handed them a gift basket. "I went with yellow since I didn't know."

Belinda threw up her hands. "You shouldn't have. The cradle was more than enough."

Smiling, Leah shrugged slightly. "I love shopping for baby things."

Belinda pulled out a soft yellow blanket and pad that fit perfectly in the cradle. There was also a matching teddy bear. "How sweet!"

"I couldn't resist."

"You wanna see my new soccer ball?" Billy asked Danny.

"Sure."

They scuttled outside.

Cal was still admiring the cradle with Matt as Belinda tucked the teddy bear back in the basket. "You three make a lovely family."

Leah started to shake her head.

"Don't you see it?"

She glanced over at Matt. "I…I'm not sure."

"Danny's dying to have a mother," Belinda confided, "and a brother or sister."

Leah felt her heart still. "Oh?"

"Yes." She smiled kindly. "I hope you won't think I'm being intrusive. I love Danny. He and Billy have been best friends all their lives. I can see you've been good for him. I've been concerned that Danny would have a hard time with this little one coming along, but with you in his life now, he's accepted it well."

"I can't take responsibility for that. Matt keeps him on an even keel."

"He's been a wonderful father, of course. But he's not a mother."

Considering her words, Leah glanced

again at Matt. The longing to tell Danny was strong.

"It bothers him when the other kids' mothers bring treats to class and he knows he doesn't have a mom to volunteer," Belinda continued. "Same thing when it was time to decide on a den mother for Scouts. They sound like small things, but no child wants to be different or left out. And every child needs a mom. Anyway, I hope things work out for all of you."

Leah tried to keep the huskiness from her voice. "Thanks."

The picture Belinda painted of her motherless child had Leah near tears. And far nearer to needing the truth to come out.

"What's the rush?" Exasperated, Matt forgot to keep his voice down.

Leah tilted her head, indicating the other diners in the café.

He lowered his voice. "Well?"

"I didn't say there was a rush, just that I'm ready to tell him. I can't see that waiting is a positive thing."

"This is awfully sudden."

"Sudden? I've been here for months now."

He remembered the increasing phone calls from Barrington, pressing him to sell the business. "Any special reason why you want to tell him now?"

"He's a little boy who needs a mother. He has one and I want him to know it."

"Why now?"

She fiddled with her iced tea. "Why not? What are we waiting for?"

"The right time."

"And who gets to decide when that is?"

He hesitated. That was a tough call, one he knew would be hard to make for either of them. "I just don't want Danny to get hurt."

"What if waiting does exactly that?"

He was torn. She could be right. Maybe Danny would feel betrayed if they kept the truth from him any longer. There was an uneasiness in Matt, though. Probably because Leah could take Danny away once he knew. But that had been possible for some time now. If she wanted Matt to move to L.A., too, why didn't she just come out with it? Why the ploys with Barrington? Did she think he'd withdraw his consent? "And what if he doesn't take the news well? What then?"

Her hands trembled. "You don't think he'll want me for his mother?"

She'd gotten to him again and he placed his hand over hers. "Leah, this news will change him forever. He's a little boy and he's going to be confused. You've got to be ready for that."

She bit down on her bottom lip. "What do you think, Matt? Do you think I'll be a good mother for him?"

He searched his heart, reached past the doubts, and surfaced with the bare truth. "Yes."

She let out the breath she'd been holding.

"You're a good man, Matt Whitaker. The best I've ever known." Her eyes fixed on him as though wanting to say more, but she didn't.

"Then I guess we're going to tell him."

She nodded, looking close to tears. "I guess so."

"There's something I have to tell you then. Danny doesn't know about John."

"I kind of figured that."

"Not because I'm ashamed of him...just that Danny's always been like my own. I'd planned on telling him when he was old enough to understand. Guess this pushes up that timetable."

"About Kyle...John, I mean. I've been thinking..."

Tensing up, he waited.

"Whenever I think about him...what he did, or might have done with Danny, well, it's based on the little time I knew him. If he'd lived, I think he probably would have eventually brought Danny back. I mean...he was young, like me. He made a rash decision, and after he'd had time to think it over, he'd have realized it wasn't the right thing to do. But he didn't have time to fix it."

That was what Matt had concluded, too, but he hadn't expected Leah to see it that way. He stared at her. There was a lot of forgiveness in this unusual woman. John had stolen eight years of her relationship with Danny because of his mistake.

Leah sighed. "And there's one other thing. He didn't like the way my parents wanted to...well...kind of control things. Since I've been here, I've spent a lot of time thinking back. You know how, as the years go by, it's easy to lose perspective? I've had it in my head that he just wasn't grateful for all the opportunities they gave him. But... he resented the fact they got to choose what they wanted him to do, where we were supposed to live. He said they'd wind up doing that to Danny, too. I was pretty much used to doing what they wanted, so I didn't see it then. But it's been clearer to see since I've been here, away from them. And now, well...I guess I just want to say how sorry I am for all the things I said about him. I know losing him hurt you."

"I want to think he'd have come to the right decision, too, but he hurt you both by his mistake. John had to have been scared once he'd taken Danny. But he lied about you leaving." Matt knew that now, even though the truth shamed him. He cleared his throat. "And I'm sorry I doubted you."

"You didn't know me then. I just showed up out of the blue."

And now?

"More coffee?" the waitress asked. "And we've got coconut cream pie. It's real good."

Leah shook her head. "Not for me."

"Three-layer chocolate cake?" the waitress asked. "It'll melt in your mouth."

Maybe so, but her sales pitch had ruined the moment.

Leah wanted everything to be perfect. Well, relaxed. She'd baked oatmeal cookies, Danny's favorite. But her hands were shaking and her neck was as tight as a stiff jar lid.

Accustomed to her coming over, Danny didn't think it was unusual for her to stop by on Saturday morning. Relax, she told herself. Keep it casual.

After they played with the dinosaur village, fed his fish and turtle, Matt joined them and they headed outside.

Matt put his arm on Danny's shoulders. "Leah and I have something to talk with you about."

"Okay."

"Why don't you sit down over here?" she asked, indicating the bench beneath the tree.

"Sure."

She ran a hand over his tousled hair. "Sweetheart, you know how your friends have mothers..." She licked her lips, so nervous her stomach was pitching. "I'm hoping you'll want a mother, too."

"Are you and Dad getting married?" he asked, bouncing up from the bench in excitement.

"No, no. That's not it."

He frowned. "Then how can you get to be my mother?"

Her voice quavered, her smile tremulous. "You'd want me to be your mother?"

Matt took over. "Danny, do you remember what I told you about your birth mother?"

Danny slowly sat back down between them. "That you didn't know where she was. But that wherever she was, she must be sad not to have a wonderful boy like me."

"Right. For a long time I didn't know where she was. And she didn't know where you were. And she was very sad to not be with you. She's been looking for you since you were born, and now she's found you."

Danny's eyebrows drew together, and he looked at them in turn.

Leah held her breath. "Yes, I've found you, Danny. I'm your mother."

"It's you?"

"Yes, sweetheart. It's me."

He looked at her in bewilderment. "How could you have lost me?"

She glanced up at Matt. "It's a very long story, Danny, but I never stopped loving you or looking for you. You have been in my heart since the day you were born." Her eyes moistened. "You're my little boy."

"But you shouldn't have *lost* me!"

Matt cleared his throat. "Danny, you know how much I love you."

Danny's voice was filled with caution. "Yeah."

"Well...you've been my boy since almost the day you were born and I've never wanted it any other way." He lowered his head, swallowing the lump in his throat. "But your natural father was my younger brother, John. He was confused when he was married to Leah, and he thought that bringing you back here was the right thing to do. Only he didn't tell Leah where he'd gone, and then he got into a real bad car accident and died."

"So, you're not my real dad?" Hurt and shock filled his quavering voice.

"In every way that matters. I've been taking care of you since you were a tiny baby. You're in my heart, Danny. I love you more than anyone else in this world."

Danny looked so betrayed, Leah felt the crumbling fragility in her own heart. "How come you didn't tell me before?"

Matt stared at him for such a long time that Leah found herself holding her breath. "I was waiting for the right time, until you were old enough to understand."

"But we never keep secrets," Danny accused.

Matt stared at him helplessly. This strong man who loved his son with all his heart. Who wanted only the best for him.

Danny jumped to his feet, storming away. When Matt didn't speak, Leah did. "Where are you going?"

"Takin' Hunter on a walk."

"We still need to talk, Danny," Leah called out.

He didn't reply.

She sighed. Maybe he needed to work some of this out by himself. "Don't go far. We'll be having lunch in about an hour."

He disappeared behind the workshop.

She slumped back on the bench. "You were right. As usual, *I* didn't think things out. Just blurted out what I wanted him to hear, not realizing...I'm sorry, Matt. Why didn't you stop me?"

"I'd have had better luck stopping a train." His voice was dull, and he stood staring into the empty space where Danny had been standing. "Don't blame yourself. I agreed with you that we'd tell him. I probably should have told him before. Maybe there never would have been the right time."

"But you thought we should wait. And I just plowed ahead." Why couldn't she have listened? Done what Matt suggested? He was the one with the parenting experience. Now Danny distrusted both of them.

Chapter Eighteen

Half an hour after lunch was ready, Danny wasn't back.

Matt called Billy's house but Danny wasn't there. "I know he's got to think this out, but we've given him long enough on his own. He won't have gone far. We'd better bring him home."

"Why don't we split up and look for him?" Leah suggested. "I've got my car. We can go in opposite directions that way, cover more ground."

Matt considered this, the pain he was feeling evident in his face and voice. "You know the popsicle stand by the Little League field? He and Billy like to hang out there sometimes. You try there first and I'll go by the Mickleson house. Maybe he's headed that way. Stay on the main roads. I can go off-road in the truck."

As Leah drove, she looked into the fields, but saw no little boy. She chastised herself for letting him sit alone with his thoughts too long. All she wanted was to find him, to put her arms around him, pour out her love and explain how very sorry she was to have hurt him. She wished she could take all that hurt on herself. It was so much worse knowing it was his.

She was tempted to take the side road to the baseball field but remembered Matt's instructions. For once, she wouldn't take off like a mad hare. But he wasn't at the field.

Then she remembered the path to the riverbank. Danny wasn't supposed to go there alone. She'd gone there with him when Matt had been with them. Feeling betrayed, angry, maybe rebellious… would he disobey his father?

Acting on instinct, she turned in that direction. The elevated riverbank was surrounded by trees, wild grass and dense scrub brush. She could only drive the small rental car to the edge of the vegetation. Then she set out on foot.

And as she walked she prayed.

Matt took the shortcut to the Mickleson home. Belinda and Cal were concerned, but sure that Danny hadn't been there.

"Do you mind if I talk to Billy alone?"

"Of course not. Whatever we can do to help."

They withdrew and Billy perched nervously on the edge of the couch.

"You know, when I was your age, my best friend was Jason Deats. Wasn't anything I couldn't tell him. Like when my dad died. That was the worst thing that ever happened. And he understood, even though he had his dad. Do you know what I'm saying, Billy?"

"I think so."

"So, if I were Danny, I think I'd come to you if something pretty big happened and I needed to talk about it."

Billy ducked his head, staring at the rug.

"I don't want Danny to get hurt."

"He won't get hurt!" Billy blurted out.

"I'm glad to hear it. You'd better tell me where he is."

"But—"

"He needs me right now, Billy. Because I love him and want only the best for him. Can you understand that?"

"I guess so. He went to the river. But he's just gonna throw rocks and stuff."

Matt patted his shoulder.

Thanking the Micklesons, he headed south. The river was a quiet place to think. One that had drawn him when he was a teen. Danny was growing up. They'd pushed that maturing process forward today. His boy was hurt and he'd be hurting for a while to come. But most of what he was feeling was confusion. It would take time for him to understand. But now, he had to face them, get over this first difficult step.

Danny looked very small when Leah spotted him. He sat on the ground, his knees drawn up, his head resting against his dog.

Leah made her footfalls deliberately loud and rustled the grass so she wouldn't startle him.

Still he jumped up, swiping at the tears that had been running down his face. He tried to keep his lips from trembling, but failed.

"Hey."

He didn't reply, gripping Hunter's collar.

"I've made a mess of things again. And I'm the grown-up. I should know better. I just got so impatient to tell you who I am."

"Moms don't lose their kids."

"Not usually, no. But I didn't have a choice. Your biological father and I were very, very young. He made a mistake."

"Why didn't you stop him?"

"He ran away. When adults run away, it's not the same as when children do. I couldn't find him. I've been looking for you for eight years. When I found out he'd died, I was so scared that meant you had, too." Her voice quavered. "But the Lord has been good, Danny. He kept you safe and gave you a wonderful father to raise you."

"Then why didn't Dad tell me?" Still feeling betrayed, he wasn't willing to give an inch.

"He was going to, sweetie, when he thought you were old enough to understand."

"I'm old enough." The lip that trembled now turned stubborn.

"Maybe. But if that's true, can't you forgive him for this one mistake?"

Danny gripped Hunter even tighter. "Do I have to pick?"

"What do you mean?"

"Between you and Dad?"

"No, never."

"Maybe he'll get tired of me someday since he's not my real father."

Leah stepped closer. "Danny, your father chose you to be his son. He *chose* you. Can you see how much that means he loves you? That he wanted *you?*"

Danny's face crumpled. Leah stepped closer, thinking she'd persuaded him. Instead he turned around, scrambling down the riverbank.

She ran to the edge. At first Danny

kept his balance, then he started skidding on the rocks. Out of control, he tumbled into the river.

Hunter barked furiously from the shore. Leah climbed down the side, then jumped into the water after her son. Waving her arms wildly, she tried to remember her swimming lessons, but all she could think of was saving Danny.

The river current swirled, splashing water over her face. The old panic was there, a hot, bubbling force, but the need to save Danny was greater.

She propelled her arms in the water and kicked her feet, but she didn't move forward. *What had they taught her in those lessons? Why had she blocked it all out in her fear?*

Danny was bobbing up and down several feet ahead of her. She reached out toward him, sinking beneath the water. Flailing her arms, she came up sputtering. Spitting out water, she shouted to Danny. "Don't worry! I'll get you."

She went under the water again. When she surfaced, she couldn't see Danny. Her heart nearly stopped.

The water covered her head again, carrying her farther downstream. She fought to get to the surface, not for herself, but for Danny. *Please, Lord, help him. Send us help.*

She broke through the water again, desperately reaching out to grab hold of something, anything to help her reach her son. But she still didn't see him. "Danny!" Her shout was more a gurgle, a plea.

Without warning she felt a rope come down over her shoulders and pull tight. Then she was being dragged to the shore. Dazed, she saw Danny sitting on the ground, Hunter licking him all over.

Matt, his face grim, pulled her with the rope until he could lift her to solid ground. She sagged against him, her breathing shallow.

"What do you think you were doing?" he yelled, shaking her.

"I—"

"You could have killed yourself. You don't know how to swim. You're scared to death of water. What if I hadn't had a rope with me in the truck? What then? What would Danny and I have done without you? Did you think about that? No. You just jumped in the river."

Her breathing was returning to normal, but she wasn't sure her hearing was. Had he said what would he have done without her?

"Danny's only eight years old. I can see how he wound up in the river. But you're a grown-up, Leah. If you're going to be a member of this family, you're going to have to start acting like one. You can't jump into a river without knowing how to swim—"

She felt a surge of indignation. "I wasn't going to let my son drown without doing something."

"No, you weren't, were you?"

She met his gaze. His eyes were tender, full of worry. She shook her head.

"Even though chances were you'd die doing it." He stroked her cheek.

She swallowed. "What was that about being part of your family?"

Matt glanced down at Danny. "We okay now, pal?"

Danny nodded, hanging on to Matt's leg.

"This isn't the most romantic setting a guy could pick, but it might be the most honest. I love you, Leah. Every stubborn inch of you. I love that you stand up for what you believe, I love that you love our son. If you'll have me, I'll do everything in my power to make sure your life is as good as the one you'll be giving up."

Forgetting her soggy clothing and drenched hair, Leah beamed as her heart started to fly. "I won't be giving up anything. I'll be getting everything."

Chapter Nineteen

Annie carried her ever growing list into the parlor. "Apple and poppyseed strudel, maybe peach, too?" Leah and Matt's reception was going to be held at Borbey House and Annie couldn't resist fussing.

"Only if we skip the entrée," Ethan replied.

Annie looked up from her clipboard and blushed. "I thought I was talking to Leah."

"Will I do?"

"You'll more than *do.*"

He took the clipboard from her and then took her hand. "We need to talk."

"Oh." Nothing good ever came of a conversation that started with those words.

But Annie put on a brave face. After all, she didn't want Ethan to be a victim of her family curse. It was better this way.

"What are you keeping from me?"

The artificial smile slid from her face. "Keeping from you?"

"I can sense it, Annie, and I don't want anything between us."

"I guess I've been fooling myself thinking I could put it off." She turned away from him, wishing she didn't have to tell him, wishing tragedy hadn't dogged her family. But he deserved to know the truth. So she told him. "And when I found out that Leah almost drowned in the river, I thought I'd caused that, too, since she insisted on being my sister."

At first he didn't say anything. She expected the usual skepticism, denial or even mocking. Instead, Ethan took her hands. "Why don't we pray about it?"

His voice was quiet but strong as he asked the Lord for His guidance to get them through this issue that troubled her, to give her peace. Then he sat beside her without speaking for a while, the familiar noises of the house and the guests around them.

Unexpectedly, a sense of peace stole into her heart. Raising her eyes, she met his. "Thank you."

"I don't ever want anything to come between us again, Annie." He lifted a strand of her dark hair. "I love you."

"You do?" Hope infused her voice like scent in a budding rose.

He smiled. "I do."

Her smile grew. "Me, too. I mean, I love you, too."

He unfastened his music insignia pin from his jacket and carefully attached it to her collar.

Her lips trembled.

"It's not a diamond ring, but until we pick one out, I'm staking my claim."

"And you're not worried about the other thing?"

"No. All I'm worried about is picking the right strudel for *our* reception."

Leah had so much to do. There were arrangements to make with her assistant to get her L.A. apartment closed and the rest of her belongings shipped to Rosewood. Then, of course, the wedding. It would be simple. Beautiful, but simple.

And she knew that together they would ask the Lord to be in this union with them. In finding Danny, she'd also found the fullness of her faith. The Lord had protected her child, given them another chance, then protected him again. She'd learned what it was to live with faith.

She felt a new sense of completeness belonging to the Community Church as well, something she'd never had before. Something she treasured.

When she'd called her parents with the news, they'd mentioned that Barrington Industries would like to buy out Matt's business and market his designs around the country, but she couldn't see him giving up his individuality. After all, anyone could go corporate. But Matt, well, he was Matt. She told him about the offer, and he agreed with her that he preferred to keep his business his own.

Annie was fussing over the wedding reception and Emma had designed an original gown. Surprisingly, the details weren't that important to Leah. She trusted Emma to make a beautiful dress. She'd just told her to keep it simple and in keeping with the surroundings. Beyond that, her energies were focused on Matt and Danny. And the blessings that just continued to flow.

The evening was ripe with honeysuckle. It was a heady scent in the damp air. White picket fences gleamed in the moonlight and couples strolled down the well-swept sidewalks.

Matt and Leah sat on the swing of the wide front porch at Borbey House.

Matt looked into her shining eyes, amazed all over again that she'd said yes to his proposal, that they were going to live right here in Rosewood. "We have some unfinished business."

Questions filled her emerald eyes. But they were questions now grounded in trust. He reached into his pocket, pulling out a well-worn jeweler's box.

She sucked in her breath. Her fingers flew to cover her mouth.

He carefully opened the old box. Inside was an exquisite emerald cut diamond. She knew, before he told her, that it had been his mother's. It was a tangible sign of the depth of his commitment, the foreverness of it. Tears filled her eyes.

"She would have loved you as much as I do." He slipped the ring on her finger. It fit perfectly. "I don't think I actually said the words the first time. Will you marry me, Leah?"

Her voice was as soft as the moonlight. "Yes. Very much yes."

Moonlight shimmered over her unfettered blond hair. Her clear eyes shone close to his, their faces a breath apart. Her lips were soft beneath his, tender, giving, whispering the love they shared.

Cradling her in his arms, he breathed in the clean smell of her hair, warming his cheek against hers and feeling her entrenchment into his heart grow ever deeper.

Sunlight pierced the tall rafters of the Community Church, casting its bounty through the stained-glass windows that dated back to Victorian times.

Leah and Matt had chosen a nontraditional ceremony. Rather than Leah walking down the aisle on her father's arm, she and Matt entered from the sides of the nave, meeting at the center. Danny served as best man and ring bearer, Annie as maid of honor. They wanted to keep the ceremony simple, to express the making of a family.

Rhonda Hunter had a hard time with what she considered the no-frills service and reception. She requested an additional reception in L.A., but Leah didn't budge. When Rhonda saw that she couldn't win, she didn't give Leah a difficult time. While she would never be a soft and cuddly mother, she had stopped trying to run Leah's life.

And Leah was ready to embark on that life.

Do you, Leah Michelle Hunter, take Matthew Andrew Whitaker... In sickness and health...for better for worse...forsaking all others...until death do you part?

She repeated the vows, her heart singing the words.

Matt stood straight and tall as he made his pledge, committing his vows to her and to God.

Blessed. The word ricocheted through his thoughts. It had been his mantra since the moment Leah had poured out her love, accepted his proposal and cried over the ring he'd given her. As it sparkled on the hand he now held, it harbored a wealth of meaning. And she'd known that instantly. This woman who had come to know his heart.

As they gazed lovingly at each other, the congregants, family and friends seemed far away.

"I do," Leah whispered again.

"Me, too," he whispered back.

"…now pronounce you man and wife. What God has brought together, let no man put asunder."

Matt looked at her tenderly, his bride/wife.

"…may kiss the bride."

Gently he touched his lips to hers, feeling her tremble. Then she smiled, that smile he loved. He clasped her hand in his, letting his strength flow to her. And together they turned to face the world as one.

Borbey House hadn't gleamed this much since its own debut. The dark walnut surfaces had been polished until shiny. Ivory lace net bunting, caught up with nosegays of yellow rosebuds, draped the doorways. Annie's family silver shone beneath the crystal chandelier.

The one extravagance Rhonda had insisted on and Leah had given in to was a small string ensemble. They played softly as a background to the sound of happy voices.

"You look incredibly beautiful, Mrs. Whitaker," Matt said.

"So do you, Mr. Whitaker," Leah replied.

Matt lifted his eyebrows. "Can men be beautiful?"

Her eyes misted. "You are."

He smoothed her cheek with the back of his hand. "And you, my love, are a gift."

The pain of their pasts slipped away,

forgotten. Only the future remained, so bright, so shiny, it reflected in the hope they saw in each other.

Danny tugged at Matt's coattail. "Dad. Is this it?"

"It?"

"Are you and Mom and me a real family now?"

Matt smiled at his bride as they each took one of Danny's hands. "Absolutely."

Danny looked up at them. "Is this just grown-up stuff now?"

The music swirled around them.

"No," Leah answered. "This first dance is for all of us." She gazed into the two faces so dear to her. "That okay with my men?"

Their chorus was music, it was wonder, it was all she ever needed to hear.

"You betcha."

* * * * *

Dear Reader,

I think there can be no greater fear than that of losing a child. For Leah Hunter, it's a loss she's lived with for eight long years. But when the search for her child brings her face-to-face with Matt Whitaker, it will take divine guidance to separate fear from fact—and one little boy from two people who love him with all their hearts.

Like most parents, stories with children touch my heart. And, also like most of you, I relish the special relationship that produces those children.

It's a tough world we live in today, but Rosewood is a gentler place where neighbors still care about one another, people matter and love flourishes. I hope you'll enjoy going there with me again.

God bless.

Bonnie K. Winn

QUESTIONS FOR DISCUSSION

1. What role does the community of Rosewood play in *Child of Mine*? Would this story have been as effective set in a large city?
2. Would Matt Whitaker have been as sympathetic had his younger brother, Kyle, still been alive, having just deserted his young family and run off? Would you have accepted him as the hero?
3. Can you relate to Annie's losses? Can you understand her genuine feeling that her family had somehow become cursed? How did you feel about her relationship with Ethan?
4. Matt's decision to allow Leah to have Danny was guided by an answer to prayer. Have you had a similarly unexpected answer from God?
5. Leah was prepared to give up everything to pursue her son, even to break a lifetime pattern of bending to her parents' will. Is this a reaction you can understand and identify with?
6. Did you come to understand Leah better as the story progressed? Did you want her to be a perfect mothering figure from the beginning? Or did you enjoy watching her grow, seeing her realize she needed Matt as a parenting partner?
7. Could Matt, Leah and Danny have been happy in the sprawling metropolitan city of Los Angeles where Leah's parents, Danny's grandparents, live? Could the trio have fit in with the faster lifestyle to have the benefit of extended family?

8. Which of the secondary characters did you enjoy the most? Some, like Emma and Tina, are from previous Rosewood, Texas, books. Do you feel like you're running into old friends when you read about them?
9. Matt was very protective of his brother's memory. Was it appropriate? And were you satisfied when he realized his brother had been wrong?
10. Was the theme of sacrifice true to the parable of the wisdom of Solomon?